A GHOST OF HER OWN

A ROMANCE

ALESSA WINTERS

DEDICATIONS

For Allen, for believing in me.

For Lisa, for constantly cheering me on.

For FTH, for always being an amazing support.

For Pat, who introduced me to fanfiction at age 8.

This book is for you.

ACKNOWLEDGMENTS

Thank you to Kristen Batko for amazing edits and notes.

Thank you to NanoWrimo for inspiring me to write in the first place.

1

And with a deep breath to fortify herself, she turns the key to the aging padlock. It crunches, somewhat concerningly so, but then the lock tumbles and she shakes off the rust dust from it with a quick twist of the wrist.

"Charming," her sister, Deborah, murmurs.

Grace gives her a quick look, before storing the padlock in her purse. "I can replace locks," she says. "Locks are the easiest thing in this entire affair to replace."

Instead of waiting for her sister to reply with yet another comment about why this entire affair is misguided and silly and such, Grace untwists the thick chain around the handle and, throwing her shoulder into it, opens the door up to the warehouse.

The warehouse.

The dilapidated, dusty, dirty, rust-filled warehouse that she's somehow, someway, going to make into a house. Or, if not a house, a place where she can live, can grow, can design, and make her own.

The air is still inside, and the dust motes balance in the beams of the setting sun, and she doesn't know if she's ever seen something so beautiful.

It's an old style split level warehouse, with half opening up to what was a grand assembly line, with a loft space and a huge bakery oven still in the middle of the massive room. Bare pipes line the walls, bringing in the plumbing and the gas for the massive oven and stoves.

Next to her, Deborah steps up, then whistles. "Grace, this place is huge," her voice is hushed, as if the expanse of the place takes all the noise and sits on it, squashing it down with its space.

Grace steels herself, then takes a deep breath and steps onto the concrete floor. Dust and rust flakes stir around her boots, but it's a familiar site, one of work and effort and her being in control of everything.

"And it's mine," she says, and her voice rings true over the space, as if it is calling her out and accepting her words. She jingles the keys in her hand. "Just mine."

Deborah cranes her neck up to the warehouse ceiling, at the exposed beams and the metal roof. "God this place will be noisy when it rains."

Grace personally prefers that, which is one of the reasons she bought it in the first place, but she's not about to say that to her easily spooked sister.

"It's waterproof, though." Grace points out, stepping further into the space. The dust motes stir around her in the sunbeams, dancing in the light from the giant windows. "I had a consulting company make sure of that, at least."

"Great. Waterproof." Deborah's brown eyes are wide as they explore the ground floor. Or, rather, she explores. Grace has been here many, many times in the process of purchasing it, this is just the first time she's been in it when it's hers.

She rests her hand on the great wood oven in the middle, and the brick is cool to her touch. The realtor had said it's been about 30 years since it's been used as a bakery, but all the equipment still works.

Instead of being used as a bakery for the last 30 years, it had been used as a factory line for children's toys and for manufacturing phone parts, until the company went under and then it had been sitting, abandoned, for the last fifteen. Thankfully padlocked and graffiti free, resting in a neighborhood behind a wealthy condo complex.

She trails her finger along the industrial stove, drawing a line in the thick dust coating everything.

The air stirs, but it's just Deborah taking a few steps back to look up on the loft.

The loft was once where the overseer's desk laid, with lovely wood flooring that's mostly escaped the ravages of time. A beautiful wooden staircase spirals up to it, drawing focus to the centerpiece of the room.

"What are you even going to do with all this space?" Deborah asks, and her voice is just as hushed as it was before. "This is like...three times the size of your old place. Four. Maybe five."

The old place was a tiny hole in the wall apartment she rented the moment she broke up with Rey, and it was awful. Claustrophobic, cramped, and full of memories of all the times he tried to win her back.

And that's not counting the last three weeks. Her lease ran out on the apartment but the sale wasn't finalized on this place, so she's been...truck living. With an air mattress and a cooler and a camp stove and way too much fast food.

Grace takes a deep breath to steel herself against all the memories hitting her. "Well, according to raw square footage, it's around seven times of that shithole." She throws a smile at her sister, who doesn't reciprocate. "I'm gonna turn that half--" she points to the area where there's already a foundation for a wall -- "into a workshop. It gets morning light, I can do all my designing and building there."

She climbs up to the loft, testing each stair as she does. Not that she hasn't tested all the stairs each other time she's been here, but still. Habits.

The wood floor shines under the dust, a quick sweep away from being perfectly clean. The thin metal railing creaks when she leans against it, but that, like all of this, can be replaced.

Deborah stares up at her, her eyebrows drawn together. "Is that even safe?"

"1930s construction, never better." She calls down. "This thing could withstand an earthquake and a tornado."

"I find that doubtful."

A flurry of movement catches her eye, in the corner of the warehouse, and she stares down.

But nothing. The air is even still, as if no one had ever disrupted it, the sun beams clear and the dust mites still. And yet, she could've sworn there was, for a brief moment, something moving. A hand waving or a limb shifting, something.

"Huh."

Grace paces the length of the loft. Which is, of course, much bigger than the entire shithole apartment. And she can see the entire floor of the warehouse, every corner, every bit of leftover machinery, every bit.

If anyone enters her home, she'll be able to see them in a second.

Good.

She smiles out at her view. "I'll put the bed up here," she calls down to her sister.

Her sister's eyes widen. "I'd get vertigo," she proclaims. "It's too...too..." she trails off, instead tossing her shiny black hair over her shoulder. "Mom would flip if she knew."

Grace nods, then dangles her feet over the edge, leaning on the metal railing. "That's why we're not going to tell her."

The unspoken truth that their mother would also immediately rat her location out to Rey hangs between them, and Deborah paces around the floor again. The furrow in her brow means that Grace should probably go back down there and comfort her, but instead she ignores her sisterly instinct and swings her feet, staring out at her new property.

She's never actually owned her own property. She went directly from her college apartments to being sequestered away in Rey's questionably legal housing complex, only able to leave for her interior design job. And once she...left...it was that tiny shithole of an apartment with only the bare bones of furniture and breathing space while she saved up every penny for this place.

Well, this place and her get out fund. For when she would inevitably have to leave, have to run, once Rey gets out of prison and inevitably tries to track her down.

The thought stirs something unhappy in her chest, as she stares down at the concrete floor below her. Maybe, just maybe, if it's secret enough and she's good enough and can fortify her house well enough, then she can stay.

But that can only happen if she gets to work.

She stands, wiping off the dust from her hands onto her work jeans. "I think I can turn this kitchen into something functional, but my camper stove is in my truck. Think you want some camp food?"

Deborah peers at her. "Are you serious?"

Grace swings herself down the stairs, a bubble of strange joy sitting inside of her, a joy she hasn't felt in ages. "Dude, I lived out of the truck, of course I have a camper stove." She tosses the truck keys to her sister, who scrambles for them. "Food's in the cooler, I'll bring in the mini fridge in a bit."

"You're not kidding." Her sister sighs, then turns to the still open door, leaving her alone in the space.

Without the other living, breathing person, the space seems to almost mold to her, and she grabs her drafting pad from where she left it the other day, when she signed the paperwork with the realtor. She flips to the rough floor plan, eyes wide, at the grid work she has before her.

It'll be magnificent.

The same flurry of movement catches her eye, in the far corner of the warehouse, where she has tentative plans on setting up a drawing table, under the vaulted windows with the morning sun.

At the moment it's in shadow, and her boot steps muffle themselves in the dust as she strides over there.

Again, there's nothing, but it's cold, in the strange corner, as if the early autumn heat wasn't reaching that far into the building.

"Huh," she says again, and it's quiet. So quiet, the sounds of traffic and the creaks of the building are gone. "Weird."

A breath of air hits her cheek, and she closes her eyes into it, cool and refreshing. While the designer part of her knows she'll have to check the wall over here for drafts and cracks, she can't quite bring herself to care at this exact moment.

For at this exact moment, she's home.

For the three seconds before her sister slams the door open, carrying the hefty camp stove that she kept in the back of her truck. "Jesus, Grace, you weren't kidding about living in there." Deborah calls out.

"It's like camping. It's fun." She takes the stove from her sister and puts it directly on the large kitchen apparatus table. "The gas to these guys are being turned on in three days, so I'll have a full kitchen then."

Deborah eyes it. "This is like an industrial kitchen, not a home kitchen sort of thing."

"Yeah, but..." Grace shrugs. "It's in fashion. There's even a Pinterest tag for this sort of thing."

"Sure." Out of a lack of anything else to say, Deborah sits on the far edge of the industrial table and watches as Grace cranks on the stove, getting out a packet of cubed steaks and a can of potatoes, and starts cooking.

Camp food is camp food, even inside a spacious warehouse.

"You're really doing this," Deborah says, muted. But her voice is muted by a bit of wonder this time. "You're really moving into here."

"I'm really moving into here." She confirms. "Thought I'd create my own space, instead of waiting for other people to do it for me."

Deborah nods, watching her. "Think you'll be safe? From him?"

And that is the question of the day. Of the month. Of the year. "I'm two states away from his prison, I think I'll make it." The bravado tastes wrong in her mouth, but she continues on. "Besides, I doubt he's going to look for me in an old Twinkies factory."

Dismay chases disbelief across her sister's face. "This place wasn't actually —"

"Nope." She pops the 'p' sound. "But it's funny to think it is."

Deborah doesn't watch the food cooking, instead stares at her sister, her attention verging on severely uncomfortable.

"This building has history, you know," Grace blurts out, shifting under her gaze. "Most warehouses like this got torn down. For apartments. In the Nineteen Nineties."

"Grace," Deborah says, and it's way more gentle than Grace wants to hear.

"And this is an amazing opportunity for me as a designer, cause I can build stuff and draft stuff in my own place and don't have to spend money on rent on a studio." She shuffles with the frying pan. "I mean, on that alone this place will have paid for itself within two years. And..." She looks at her sister and immediately wishes she hadn't, for her sister has that disappointed look all over her face. "And if I need to I can section off parts and rent it out. For extra money. In case my job commissions go away."

Deborah sighs, and it's the sigh of a sister who thinks she knows way better. "I'm not gonna talk you out of this, I'm not even gonna try," she says, her voice weary. "I just don't want you to...I dunno...think this is a savior. Think this will solve all your problems. Think this will make Rey go away."

And that stings, but it's also something she's thought of before. "I have to try something, though."

Her sister purses her lips, then looks at her watch in a very obvious way. "I'm supposed to meet Greg for dinner," she says, slow. "So as much as I like camp food," her voice makes it clear she doesn't want camp food. "I don't think I should stay."

Grace saw that one coming the moment her sister called it charming. "Well, you'll have to come out again when I have it put together."

Her sister circles around the giant table and gives her a too tight hug from behind, careful to not get in the way of the cooking. "Of course I'll do that." She buries her face in Grace's back, squishing her nose in her shoulder blades, like they used to do when they were kids and scared from movies, or as she did when Grace first ran to her from Rey and was too frightened to sleep on her own and instead crashed on her sister's bed, and it's such a moment of comfort that Grace closes her own eyes for a split second, ignoring the sizzle of the camp stove.

They stay like that for a breath, before Deborah pulls away, and Grace tries not to miss it too much.

"You're staying here overnight?" Deborah asks, and her voice sounds like she was tearing up as well.

"Yeah, I'll be safe."

"But how will you sleep?"

Grace looks across the dusty ground, across the rust filled floor and the giant industrial kitchen. "My air mattress is pretty good."

Deborah wrinkles her nose at her. "Mom would flip."

"I'm getting my bed delivered tomorrow, it'll go up in the loft."

After a moment, as if steeling herself to do so, Deborah nods, then pats her sister on the back, heading out and leaving Grace all alone with the camp stove and the setting sun.

2

Thank god the bare wiring will work as soon as she replaces the lightbulbs.

Thank god she knows enough to have a ladder and an extra packet of lightbulbs in her truck.

Out of an abundance of paranoia, she moves her truck inside the warehouse with her. It's not that the truck is the most distinctive vehicle ever, but just enough of Rey's friends and associates know she has the truck and they might drive by.

Somehow.

Even though this is pretty much the exact opposite neighborhood that they run in and, as far as she knows, they aren't actively looking for her. Yet.

She drags the air mattress out of her truck bed and up the spiral stairs into the loft. If she's gonna make that her own bedroom, might as well start sleeping in it now. Can't make a home without staying in it, as complicated as it is to do so on this first night.

After sleeping every night in the claustrophobia of her truck, the expanse of the room is vast, and she works up a sweat pumping up the air mattress with the foot pump.

The setting sun trickles through the large windows, bathing the floor in soft pinks and oranges, mixing with the rust and the grime of the years and diffusing it, making it gentle and glorious. It takes away her breath, for just a second.

And yet, her skin crawls. It's like someone's watching, like she's somehow not alone, but...

But even in the yellow light of the cheap bulbs that somewhat flicker in the inconsistent electricity, she can see everything in the warehouse from her vantage point. And there's no one.

Hours later, when the only light she keeps on her little reading lamp next to her air mattress, she wakes from her sleep with a jerk.

For a second she just stares up at the ceiling, so vaulted and far away that she can barely see it, her pulse racing. Her legs are slick with sweat inside her heavy duty sleeping bag, and she kicks it off of her, feeling her heart beat so hard it's practically behind her eyeballs.

The reading lamp casts deep shadows through the warehouse, catching on the dim shape of her truck and the giant industrial kitchen. The chimney juts up, a dark monolith of brick and metal that leaves inky black shadows behind it.

Using her phone as a flashlight, she aims it at the door. The rolling garage style door is still down, so no one could've gotten in. The windows are all closed and too high for anyone to get into without the help of ladders on both sides.

And yet, her heart still pounds.

"Okay," Grace whispers, hugging her knees to her chest. "Okay, this is a thing."

Something creaks, and she closes her eyes, but nothing more. "Right. New place."

She sits on the air mattress for a few seconds, feeling foolish. This place is safe. There's no one else. For all she knows, this place could have mice and they're just trying to get at her leftover camping food.

Though the realtor swore that wasn't the case, but eh. Realtors lie all the time. That's why she works in interior design--she can catch them before anything gets too far.

Another creak, and she squeezes her eyes shut, before uncoiling her legs and slipping her feet into her sandals. She'll feel better if she checks it out, she just knows, no matter how silly she feels at the moment.

And if her paranoia has taught her anything, it's that it's better to check things out when she has suspicions than to let them grow. Cause if she lets them grow without acting on them, they're either things that ruin relationships or things she should have been wary of to begin with.

It's tough to not draw the connection to Rey and all his dealings, but she shoulders that thought with her reading lamp, picking it up and dialing it up.

The warm glow spreads, not enough to combat the shadows, but just enough that there's the vague...shape. Of something. In the corner with the draft.

Her heart jumps into her throat.

"Hello?"

The sound of her voice echoes out through the warehouse, before dying suddenly, as if it had never existed.

The shape jerks, as if scared by the noise, before it vanishes.

And that's the right word for it, she reflects as she stares at the corner. There was once an inky black shadow, and then there isn't one now, just the bare brick.

She tries to swallow, then swallows again, not entirely certain she's not asleep. The back of her neck crawls, so she shuffles up and down the winding stairs, the metal of the hand guards chilled against the air.

"Hello?" She calls out again, while flipping the switch to all her faulty wiring and janky light bulbs. They flicker, but...

But nothing.

She's just as alone as she thought she was, and everything feels vaguely like someone is playing a prank on her.

~

THE NEXT DAY she feels less like someone was playing a prank on her and way more like she's a silly little girl who just lets her imagination run rampant all over her.

It's not a great feeling.

But a job is a job, and she has to meet clients at their place with her completed sketches for their newly lit great room, so she rolls up the garage style door, backs out her truck, then rolls it down and padlocks the doors with her new lock.

If she's gonna park her car in here all the time she needs to automate at least part of this.

The early autumn air bites into her cheeks, but she cranks the window down on her truck, desperately trying to use the cold to wake up. It's usually better than any coffee, but today it just makes her eyes water up.

The job itself is easy. Not mindless, but dealing with an appreciative client and a very competent lighting and electrical designer, Trixie.

After the meeting, Trixie and her walk back to the cars and they couldn't be more different: Trixie's sleek sedan against Grace's beat up truck with a cover.

"Are you okay?" Trixie asks, as soon as they're out of earshot and away from the client's front door. "Usually you're more..." She waves her hand, effusive.

Grace shrugs, twirling her truck keys in her hands. "Got a new place, haven't adjusted yet."

Trixie's eyes light up, because she's just as much of an interior designing nerd as Grace is, despite being mostly a lighting technician. "New place?"

And for a split second Grace thinks about bringing Trixie back, having her fix the futzing lights and double check all the wiring instead of doing it herself, but...

But Grace can't say, beyond a shadow of a doubt, that Trixie doesn't know Rey.

It's fucked up, the sort of scenario that she's in, where she has to doubt her colleagues and everyone around her, but still.

"It's a cool new space, still working on it," Grace says, as a deflection, "Not ready to show anyone yet."

Trixie shrugs, tossing her shiny blond hair over her shoulder like it's the easiest thing in the world. "No new place ever is." She digs her own keys out of her too nice purse. "If you need any help, or want any unsolicited tips, just let me know, I'll give you all the annoying advice." She pauses, her eyebrows wrinkling. "New space? Is it even built?"

"Sorta?" Grace smiles, unlocking her truck door as if that might actually stop Trixie from asking questions.

The look in her eyes is definitely not satisfied, but Trixie gets into her own car, leaving Grace to breath too hard in her truck for a few seconds before pulling down the overly fancy driveway.

While Trixie isn't someone she'd call a friend, as she lives way down in the city proper and is too far away for her to properly hang out, she is someone who Grace enjoys working with. Someone who could be a friend, given proximity and honesty.

And, well, honesty has bitten her in the ass too much before, which is how she ended up in this sort of situation to begin with. And she has no intention to going back to living in a cramped apartment full of fear, so she feels she's owed some privacy.

THIS TIME, when she rolls up the door to her place so she can drive in, it's like the very walls are angry.

The rolling door, so much like the storefronts of old, creaks unbearably, and she puts oil on the list of things she'll need.

With the ever present smell of dust and rust hitting her, she blinks, just a bit too rapidly. It's already feeling like it's a bit of home, like the place is already calling to her with the smell.

The light streaming in from the windows casts the place in a bit of a daze, a soft hazy light too pretty to not love.

In the corner, near that cold spot and the ambiguous thing she may or may not have seen last night, stands...someone. A figure. A person. Maybe.

She freezes, the padlock still in her hand, and the entire building creaks around her.

"Hello?" She calls out again, feeling foolish, like that little child again.

With that in mind, she keeps her eye on the figure, and opens her truck door again, fishing around blindly for the shotgun she keeps under the seat.

Cause she's had too many run ins with too many people to not have a shotgun in her truck. Not that she's actually shot anyone with it, or shot anything besides paper with it, but still.

It's a familiar, heavy weight in her hands, the wood grooved and textured to her. Back when she just got away from Rey, she took it with her everywhere, and practiced at a tiny gun range every day.

She might be imagining it, but the figure turns towards her. Still featureless, with shoulders that are broad but lacking in distinction.

Gun in her hand, butt against her shoulder, she steps forwards. "Who's there?" She tries to school her voice to be strict, but it still wavers embarrassingly.

The figure stays put, then, faltering, as if injured, takes a step forward. As if he (or she, but she's betting on he) forgot how to bend his knees, and had to unstick his shoes.

Something in the faltering step triggers the sympathy instinct in her, because of fucking course it did, and she's been taken down too many times to let it take her now.

"This is private property, you're trespassing." She takes a step closer, into one of the beams of light from the windows, and...

The figure, now only thirty feet away from her, vanishes.

Just like the night before. Just like how it happened in that weird haze of little sleep and paranoia of the middle of the night.

She blinks, casting her eyes around the warehouse. Nothing's changed, nothing's disturbed, her sleeping bag is still bunched up on the loft on the now deflated air mattress.

And there was someone there, but now he is gone.

Taking another deep, steeling breath, she fits the butt of the shotgun back into her shoulder and stalks forward, to where the figure once stood.

Cold air smacks her face, pushing some of her now tangled black hair away from her face, and she shivers at the sudden burst.

"Ooookay..." she whispers, relaxing her grip on the shotgun. "This is..."

The air moves around her face, a small vortex of something that's not quite wind but not quite a breeze. It's not violent, per say, but it feels purposeful. Odd.

And there's still no one else in the building and still no one else in the spot, just an odd bit of cold.

She stands there, her feet tingling and her heart pounding, before she gives up and finally moves her truck into its space.

SHE SPENDS the rest of the day wrestling with her friend's shop vac and cleaning up the decades of dust, revealing the beautiful hard concrete floor that's somehow in fashion now, but only with large area rugs and bright furniture.

Which, of course, she's bought some. She's a designer, she knows how to dress the area, and as she surveys the now somewhat cleaned up space, a small pit of wonder fills the bottom of her stomach. A small pit of wondering how she can deserve this, and how she could make this happen.

The same pit that tells her she'll fail, that it'll break apart, and everything will turn out horrible. The same pit that tells her she'll end up at that complex of a house with Rey again and not be able to leave but for limited work.

She takes a deep breath, and the warehouse smells of being freshly vacuumed. It's a scent she usually associates with work, with a shop, with construction, and her doing things of her own ability. It's a smell of her being in control, so she takes another deep breath, and another.

It's the very beginning of dusk, where the sky starts to dim just a bit and the first strip of orange appears at the horizon, and the light streams in pretty pink right when someone officially knocks on her door.

Well, knocks on the outer door, and it takes her a moment to wrestle up the rolling door before getting to the actual door.

It's three delivery men, all wearing uniforms and with IDs that match the ones the company gave her when she ordered the delivery, so she lets them in, her heart pounding, stashing the shotgun next to the door.

The tall delivery man gives it a raised eyebrow, but no one comments on it.

The shorter of the three men gives a whistle when he sees the space. "You gonna actually live here?" He says, handing her the delivery clipboard for signatures.

She nods, scribbling her signature in the proper places, keeping one eye on the open warehouse doors. "You can drive in the truck if it'd be easier," she says, even though the vague idea leaves her skin crawling.

The shorter man looks at his compatriots and shrugs. "Much thanks, Ma'am, but we're backed right up to the front."

They bring in her large area rugs and splay them out, then her two couches, one for her living area and one for the workshop, and her large sketching table, and she watches them struggle to get the large bed frame up the spiral staircase.

Out of spite, she places a large, vibrantly deep red overstuffed armchair right in the cold space, with the single fuzzy rug she ordered underneath it. A place where, if she gets over her imagination and her paranoia, will probably be super pleasant to read during the hot summers.

And she resolves to do that. To get over this, spend as much time reading there as she damn well pleases, so she can get over this. She got away from Rey, she can get over a cold spot and some childish scares to read.

The deep red of the chair blends in beautifully with the brick wall, and, if not for the creepiness, it'd be her favorite place in her new house.

As the delivery men trickle out, the entire warehouse creaks again, as if shuddering off their influence. And, as she closes the rolling gate, it's like the entire place heaves a sigh.

Now lit entirely by the flickering light bulbs, it at least looks like a place that a real human lives in. With furniture and everything. Her giant mattress is still encased in plastic, but...there's stuff in it now. At least.

She flops over on one of her new couches, the microsuede soft against her face, and squeezes her eyes shut.

It doesn't echo anymore inside, and that small change to the feel of the warehouse is everything. Instead of some large foreign space, it's...inhabited.

As if sensing her words, the entire place shudders again, the familiar creak of a building built before modern times.

"I know, I know," she says, rolling over and staring up at the vaulted ceiling. The couch is way, way too comfortable. "I'll get the wiring redone, you'll feel better when I do."

If she doesn't focus on it, the lightbulb under the loft looks like it's swinging softly, but when she turns her head to take a glance it's still.

"I'll even modernize the piping, if I need to." Though the exposed piping is something she loves dearly, and attracted her to the space in the first place.

And...she's talking to an empty warehouse.

With the shotgun laying unceremoniously on the floor rug next to the couch, she squeezes her eyes shut again, breathing out hard.

It's not like she thinks she's the pinnacle of mental health--the fact that she bought a warehouse and is immediately living in it says something not so complimentary, but she never spoke to herself in the tiny little shithole of an apartment or the complex house of Rey.

Not that she spoke much at all in that complex. Which is, of course, part of the point.

The air moves, almost lazily, over her face, but she ignores it, drifting off on the couch instead of climbing the spiral stairs to her still plasticked bed.

AGAIN, like clockwork, she jerks awake, and all the lights in her tiny little warehouse are swinging on their cords, flickering in and out.

She pushes herself up onto her elbows, staring around with the sort of dumb glance of someone woken from too deep of a sleep.

The lightbulb over her makeshift kitchen swings, perilously close to falling off, and she scrambles up.

"Okay, okay," she mutters, reaching up to grab it to stabilize it. It's cool, too cool in her hand.

And, as she just lets it rest, cool and flickering in her hand, she stares out at her space, eyes searching for that brief glance of movement.

But, because of the changing shadows of the swinging bulbs and the flickering into darkness then back to the yellow light, she can't see anything.

Heart pounding, she backs up to the couch, sitting down and resting a hand on the shotgun, her mind racing.

Everyone would laugh at her, and she might lose what little support and belief she has from her few friends who know her past, but the hair on the back of her arms rises up.

She hasn't believed in ghosts since she was a little kid, and with Rey she learned that the worst monsters are the ones right in front of you, but man. This is some horror movie stupid effects shit.

And she knows, she knows that it's irrational, but as she hugs her knees to her chest on her brand new couch and stares at the swinging lights, she doesn't know what else to think.

Did she somehow buy a haunted warehouse?

3

"Haunted is a bit beyond you, don't you think?" Deborah says, stirring the fake sugar into her iced tea with only a raised eyebrow to show what she truly thinks.

Grace hugs herself, playing with the edges of her braid. "I mean, there's some spooky shit, I know that, but...yeah. It's weird."

Chasing a feeling of normalcy or something, she felt that it would be smart to go visit her sister in the city. Since her sister came out to the suburbs to see her, it was only fair.

Though the open air diner gives her the creeps. Too many people walking around, too many people she doesn't know milling behind her.

"It could be near a railway line?" Deborah suggests, clinking her spoon against the glass a few too many times. "Or, I dunno, really sensitive to big trucks driving on the streets?" Her lips quirk up into a smile. "And, you know, regular old building drafts causing the coldness?"

"And that figure? Who vanished?"

She sighs, finally setting down her spoon and moving her iced tea to the side to embrace Grace's hands in her own. "You've always been over imaginative, Gracie," she says, and her voice is gentle, way more gentle than reasonable. "This could be one of those times."

Her words sting, of course, but all Grace does is look away, cause really, she doesn't have much in the way of proof to argue with her sister. "I wasn't being over imaginative with Rey," she counters, but even she knows that is a cheap shot.

Deborah scrunches her nose at her. "And he's in prison, so I don't think that counts."

Feeling the back of her neck crawl, Grace cranes her neck to look around while her sister studiously ignores her doing so.

THAT NIGHT, despite her heart pounding when she settles herself into her huge new bed, nothing happens.

She doesn't know if she feels disappointed or not.

THE NEXT NIGHT, as she nestles deep into her brand new down coverlet, with the too high thread count sheets almost caressing her, her heart starts to pound.

She opens her eyes, but remains still otherwise. The last few times, when this started, she had been asleep...but now her heart pounds and she;s wide awake.

The dim reading lamp doesn't illuminate much, just a yellowed glow over the loft. The wooden floors almost appear slick, like oil has spilled over and covered it with a luminous sheen.

A breath of cool air hits her face, like a tentative touch. Breathing out of her nose, she pushes herself to her elbows.

The loft is empty.

Of course.

A shiver of disappointment winds its way up her spine, cause the last thing she wants is to be wrong about something again. Not that she particularly wants to be inhabiting a haunted warehouse, but she wants to be wrong even less.

So she sits up fully, the sheets pooling around her legs, and she wishes she had gone to bed in something more protective than a cami and terrycloth shorts.

She lifts the reading lamp up further, the warm light spilling down to the floor below, but not enough with the still unfamiliar shadows of her new furniture.

"Right," she whispers.

A hand on the rickety railing, she descends the spiral staircase, one step at a time. It's cool underneath her feet, but it's the normal cool of the early autumn nights.

A twitch of movement in the far corner, and that fission of disappointment flips to something between satisfaction and fear.

She lifts the reading lamp higher, and the light pools around her. But, because of the strange feeling quelling around her, she keeps her lips sealed.

For the figure had disappeared when she had asked that question, and it might be nothing...but...

She steps from the stairs to the bare concrete, rough against the bottom of her feet, the warehouse looming large in front of her, foreign and gaping.

Breathing deep, she steps into the room at large, the meager light her only source of contact, her skin feeling every tiny movement in the air around her.

Down here, on the same level, there's the same figure, standing by the chair. She squints and can see the bare outline of his hand, touching the fabric, as if it puzzles him. He -- she assumes -- runs his hands over and over the soft over cloth, as if unaware that she is even there, that she is even standing and approaching him.

Keeping her footsteps light, but the light higher, she inches forward, and he becomes more distinct. Sharpens.

She can see a bare edge of a nose, like a shadow on a silhouette, and a trace of a jawline. Hair, cropped close against his skull, and deep-set eyes.

Eyes still focusing on the armchair, as if he cannot sense the light changing around him, as if this tiny change in the world is all that matters, and she creeps up until she is only a dash away, a mere seven feet, and the light from the small reading lamp illuminates him fully.

There's something soft, indistinct around his edges, and her heart pounds faster, harder, a raucous patter inside her chest, and she gasps, a quick intake of breath.

At that his head snaps up, over, and she meets his eyes. They're crystal blue, piercing, not of this world, and he looks caught, as if he is doing something entirely unacceptable. As if he is trespassing.

She blinks at him, and he doesn't move.

"Hello?" She whispers, unable to help herself. "Are you...are you okay?"

He seems to pause, like those computer simulations where the video glitches out, and his very...being...flickers.

Instead of that fear from just a few moments ago, a strange calm steals over her, like this thing can't hurt her.

She can't know if it'd -- if he'd -- be able to hurt her, but her instincts, her instincts that have done her wrong so many times, tell her she's safe.

"Are you a ghost?"

He mouths something back, a bare hint of his lips moving, but no sound. A perplexed look crosses his face, as if he knows he had meant to speak but nothing came out.

She holds the lamp between them, fully illuminating his face.

It's...handsome, in a way. In the way that things can be utterly still and utterly unreal, but still fit the generic idea of what handsome is. His eyes bore deep into hers, and his jawline is defined and almost delicate, but his shoulders are broad and his features even.

Even in processing them in her brain, she doubts that 'even features' is really a phrase for handsome.

"I'm Grace. Grace Reddy," she says, feeling oddly rude for not introducing herself earlier. To a possible ghost. In the warehouse she bought with cash and rightfully owns.

The ghost person nods, almost thoughtful, and mouths something back, before flickering a few times and reappearing a few steps away.

"Are you okay?" She asks, her heart pounding at the sudden movement.

She's not sure if she's imagining it in the dim light, but she thinks she sees him rolling his eyes.

He flickers, again, a profoundly frustrated look on his face, before he's suddenly, suddenly, way too close. Inches away from her face.

She jerks back, stumbling and dropping the reading lamp. It doesn't break, because it's actually a modern device and not something out of a gothic novel, but it rolls away, tucking itself behind the overstuffed chair, leaving them with shadows and the vague outlines of each other.

She imagines she can feel his breath on her skin, but in reality there's just a creeping cold, biting into the apples of her cheeks and the tip of her nose.

Almost out of some leftover instinct from Rey, she puts a hand up in between them, something to push away and —

A flurry of movement, and her hand goes so cold it's almost numb, before the vague sensation of someone holding her hand back.

In the dim light, she looks down, and he's cradling her hand in his. It's not the feeling of someone actually touching her, but much softer. Like vapor, or more like a meringue. A soft dough, something not quite liquid and not quite solid, something with a lot of air in it.

She snaps her eyes up to his, and he looks just as surprised as her, before he vanishes.

Vanishes and doesn't reappear.

Her heart thudding, she slowly bends over and retrieves the lamp, but sees no one else in the warehouse but her.

Hands shaking, outside of her control, she collapses into the overstuffed armchair, pulling the throw blanket on top of her. She's shuddering, like she does when she cries or when she's too angry to think, but...

Okay. So she totally does have a ghost.

She can work with this.

4

S o once she decides that yes, she has a ghost, and yes, there is some sort of paranormal fuckery mumbo jumbo going on, she sees the asshole everywhere.

Out of the corner of her eye, when making scrambled eggs on her comically large industrial stove, as if he is peering at her. Observing her.

Hovering over her shoulder as she rolls up the interior door so she can roll out her truck and actually, you know, go to work.

Up in the loft, as she stares at the pile of clothes half unpacked but still on top of her suitcase, still in her terrycloth shorts and tank top from the night before. He stands there, blinking at her, before flickering out and disappearing again.

At least it isn't when she's naked. At least when she's caught him.

It's a mild frustration, with him not appearing long enough for her to try to speak to him, or communicate, just give her the vague feeling of being under too much surveillance and with too many people in her space.

Her wide, cavernous space.

So, when it comes time for her to actually get down and redo the wiring up to the loft, she's grumpy. The type of grumpy that she knows isn't reasonable, she knows isn't productive, but whatever. Still grumpy.

She's on her ladder under the loft positioning the cable staples with her brand new non-flickering non metallic sheathed cables to the reinforced floor, when she sees him flicker into being out of the corner of her eye.

"Yeah, I see you over there, laugh it up," she mutters. She's grimy, covered in concrete dust and sawdust and probably five other types of dust as well. It's sticky work, and her little tiny fan she has plugged into the socket isn't helping nearly as much as it is just pushing around more types of dust around.

This time, he doesn't flicker away like all the other times, instead cocking his head and staring at her hands as she measures, shifts the ladder another 54 inches, and puts in another fastener.

This type of wiring isn't her favorite type, but it's far from the worst, and it's well worth it to have a proper light switch and lighting tracks in her room.

She runs the cable up the side, and he draws her eye once more. He's still, almost unmoving, and entirely inhuman, and as she drags her noisy metal ladder across the concrete ground, she gets no more reaction than the quick blink blink of his eyes at her.

Like she's the one who isn't supposed to be here.

It digs at something deep in her, something hard fought inside her psyche, the part of her that wrestled control of herself from the chaos that was Rey and established her own method to her own madness, and now this ghost is just...staring at her.

Instead of climbing back up the ladder, she squares her shoulders at him, and is rewarded by another still face blink blink.

"Why are you here?" She asks, blunt.

Slowly, ever so slowly, as if he is imitating a bad horror movie, his head tilts to the side. As if he thinks it will intimidate her.

It does, but only in the way that shores up the weird wave of anger inside of her.

"You can hear me, yes?" She asks, taking a step closer.

His head jerks down, almost an approximation of a nod.

Her pulse jumps, at that direct bit of communication. "And you're just...here?"

She's rewarded with a narrowing of his eyes and a casual lift of a shoulder. It's not the friendliest of motions, but not the least friendliest either.

"Are you...are you angry?" It seems like the thing to ask, of a ghost in her house that she just acquired.

Again, the narrowing of the eyes, slimming the incredible ice blue down to slits. But, obviously, he says nothing, not even opening his mouth to attempt this time.

"Right," she mutters, and adjusts the metal ladder up with a creak, grabbing one of her light fixtures that she wants to set up on the side of the floor of the loft. She's proud of it, in the way that someone can be proud of something she bought. It's wrought iron with many light bulbs on it, fitting right in with the industrial nature of the warehouse.

She bought it the day after she put in the offer for this warehouse, with the hope and prayer she would get it and be able to actually live here.

And now she's here, wrestling with a fixture that's probably meant to be handled by two experienced people all by herself, and he's just...watching.

"Can you actually touch things?" She calls over her shoulder as she teeters on the ladder, holding one edge of the lighting fixture in place with her hip.

She gets a blink, and a slow shake of the head.

"I saw you touching the couch, thought you might be able to help and —"

The light bulb closest to her POPS, showering her with glass dust.

She flinches, turning her face away just in time, shutting her eyes and somehow keeping her balance on the ladder. She sways, for a brief second, before opening her eyes again, and staring at the shards of glass now falling to the ground.

"Oh." She coughs, and looks back.

He stares at her, stricken, his mouth agape, as if he had no idea what he had just done.

She breathes, hard, out of her nose. "Oh."

So THE NEXT day she sits in a too crowded Starbucks and tries to google ghostbusters. Except, you know, without actually typing in ghostbusters because of protected movie properties that clogged up the links and made it so it was almost impossible to find anything.

After trying "paranormal investigator" and "ghost hunter" and "seance conductor," she settles on spiritual house cleanser and spends a few hours enjoyably scrolling through crackpots posting about how their reiki will make the energy of a house flow better and how they can heal with ancient runes.

But, after the first few pages of tumblr blogs and too-edgy-for-you pagans, there's a collection of links that give her something resembling hope.

Finally, after too long wasting time on her own amusement, she finds a link to a list of "trusted extra-normal spiritual consultants" and even a few who claim to specialize getting rid of unwanted spirits in houses, sets up some appointments for herself, and heads to her client meeting.

THE FIRST ONE comes by that evening after a brief call, and it's with too much nervousness that she rolls up the interior door to let them in.

It's a young man, with a fresh face and beautiful hazel eyes, wearing clothes that would be more fit for a construction zone than a house call.

He steps inside, raising an eyebrow with a whistle while he looks at her space. "Dang, this all yours?" He carries a briefcase, and it's the most incongruous thing of this entire affair.

Grace nods. "I'm Grace, we spoke on the phone?"

He doesn't really look at her, just cranes his neck to look at the space. "You said there was a ghost? Of a man?"

She leads him to the giant industrial stove and oven, and he unceremoniously plonks down his briefcase, snapping it open.

Inside are a plethora of herbs and bundles of sticks, and a variety of small bags and sachets. The boy -- he's probably younger than her so she has an issue calling him a man -- leafs through it, as if she no longer exists.

As if summoned, the ghost appears, close to her left elbow, leaning over to stare in the briefcase with something approaching confusion.

And she hasn't seen him since he exploded the lightbulb, so she levels him with a glare, which he absolutely doesn't respond to.

"Is that stuff supposed to get rid of him?" She asks.

The ghost turns and gives her just the most offended look, but it's a comical offended look, not the icy cold stare of the night before.

The boy nods. "He probably already tried to run away since I got here, carrying this load in here. Where is the ghost the worst?"

She and the ghost exchange a glance. "Worst?"

"Where does he appear the most, bother you the most, that sorta thing. I'm going to create a block, so he can't come in that way again."

The ghost peers closer at the briefcase, reaching out and trying to touch it. His hand just falls through it, passing through it like it's nothing. Of course.

It's also the first time she's seen him do that.

"Well, now he appears sort of everywhere, but it used to be by that chair?" She jerks her thumb over to it, and again, the ghost gives her a raised eyebrow.

He's much clearer, today, then he had been in the past. Not as transparent. Almost...almost like the third person in the room, and it's fucking unreal.

"And is he over there now?" The boy asks, pouring some dried herbs into a satchel and picking up what she assumes is a bundle of sage. She's seen too much cheesy TV to not identify that bundle easily.

Again, she exchanges a glance with the ghost. "No, he's right...there." She points to where the ghost is still halfway leaning through the stove to look at the briefcase.

He gives her a dirty look and wrinkles his nose at her.

The boy blinks at her, slowly, as if unable to comprehend what she's saying. "Nah, I would've sensed him." He shrugs, then takes the sage bundle and lights it, waving it halfheartedly in the direction she pointed at, then stalking over to the chair.

The smoke lazily lifts its way through the ghost, and he just locks eyes with her, as if to mock her for trying this shit.

The pungent smell of the sage burns the back of Grace's throat, but like hell she's gonna show that.

"What's in the packet?" She calls out, flopping onto her large couch. Her ghost stays near her, and she would say he was hovering near her, but as he is a ghost that would be inaccurate. He's hovering like an annoying mother would, not how the stereotypical ghost is said to hover.

"Sage, salt, lavender, charcoal, loads of pepper and vinegar, shit like that," he calls back, casual, and she feels incredibly dumb for inviting him into her house.

And paying him for doing this in her house.

"And that's supposed to keep a ghost away?" She asks, her eyes falling onto the ghost in question right next to her.

He raises an eyebrow at her, as if mocking the very idea of what she's doing. Which, at this point, seems fair.

"He's probably already running ascared," the boys says, waving the sage around the chair like it's some sort of magic wand. "Do you have a draft over here? It's awfully cold."

Again, she locks eyes with the ghost, and slowly, ever so slowly, the ghost smiles. It's not exactly a comforting smile, more of the smile of someone who wants to start some shit and be incredibly annoying while doing so.

"Oh god," she mutters, letting her head thump back on the couch.

The ghost pushes himself away from the couch, somehow not passing through that, and stalks over to where the boy is still waving the sage around. The look on his face, no longer blank, is mischievous, and in any other situation she'd foolishly find it charming, but now it's probably one of the more intimidating things she's seen all year.

"Don't harm him," she calls out.

The boy looks back at her, surprised. "Oh, this doesn't harm any ghosts, it just makes them go somewhere else, don't worry." The ghost passes his hand through the boys face, back and forth, and the boy shivers. "I don't hurt ghosts, I just kick them out of their homes." He shivers again, otherwise completely unaware of the ghost touching him.

Silently, the ghost looks back at her, nods once, then continues annoying the boy.

It verges on comical, and she rolls her eyes. "Right. Do what you must." And she really can't tell who she's talking to.

AFTER THE BOY LEAVES, the ghost comes back over to her, looking far too amused for someone who's supposed to be banished by some smelly herbs.

She lolls her head over to look at him, and he's all but leaning over her couch, somehow not going through it like he did the boy's briefcase. "That didn't work."

He shakes his head, his eyes light like she's never seen them before. He opens his mouth and speaks, but nothing comes out.

She shakes her head back. "Couldn't hear you."

He rolls his eyes, and the amount of energy and animation seems to be at a direct conflict with the amount of fucks she gives at this moment.

"I only called him because you exploded the lightbulb," she explains, and a small part of herself knows it is the voice she uses to explain things to small children or animals.

He looks around the place, and the setting sun is filling the space with a warm glow of pinkish light from the high vaulted windows, and it's like he's seeing it for the first time.

"Did...did those herbs make you stronger?"

He half shrugs, wanders off, standing near the corner and the chair, where the worst of the sage stink lingers.

Grace pushes herself up, closes and locks the door, then rolls down the inside door with a clatter. If she's going to talk to this ghost thing, she's just going to go crazier than she already is, and that's not going to be good for anyone. "Has anyone else ever seen you?"

Without looking at her, he nods.

She padlocks the rolling door. "Great."

⁓

THE NEXT PERSON she brings in gets so scared by the 'presence inside her house' that they leave and refuse payment, leaving Grace feeling more foolish than ever and the ghost giving the best impression that he's laughing.

He's much more distinct, now, and Grace gets the creepy crawly feeling that it's because she's in the warehouse.

⁓

THE THIRD PERSON she brings in is a tiny redhead hipster girl named Heather who wears far too many scarves for someone this early into the autumn season.

The moment Grace rolls up the interior door, her eyes go wide, but it's not the going wide at her space that Grace has gotten used to.

"Wow," she breathes, stepping gingerly over the threshold. "You...really got yourself a ghost."

Grace hesitates at the door, watching the waif of a woman tentatively step forward, her eyes zeroing in on the chair in the corner.

The ghost hasn't shown himself today, but she's not certain if that's intentional on his part or not, so she's been mostly ignoring the lack of otherworldly companion and gotten a lot of drywall done.

"I haven't seen him yet today," she says, rolling the door back down with a clank.

Heather jumps at the noise, eyes wide, before turning back to the room. "You see him often?" She nestles her hand into her oversized messenger bag, as if that can save her from whatever is out there.

Grace nods, then feels a smidgen foolish, cause the woman isn't looking at her at all. "More now. I used to only see him at night, and only in silhouette. Now...it's like a person, and his eyes are all weird."

Heather turns back to only raise an eyebrow at her, before shrugging. "Alright," she says simply. "That happens a lot, don't stress about it."

Out of a lack of anything to do, Grace follows Heather around as she slowly paces to the far corner.

"Did you put the chair there?" Heather points.

"Yeah, it's always cold there, thought it'd be nice in the summer." Grace steps around some of the drywall, erected in a half wall around the work area, and feels a little bit of pride. It almost looks like the construction was on purpose, like it was meant to happen, instead of just a collection of construction materials.

Heather pauses, right on the edge of the fluffy white carpet. "Can I step on this?"

It's such an odd question that Grace wrinkles her eyebrows. "Yes? Of course?"

Heather flaps her hand at her. "I wasn't really asking you."

The hair on the back of Grace's arms rises. "You can...talk to him?"

"Sorta." Heather seesaws with her hands. "It's much more of a...I can get vague sense? Sorta a yes or no sorta thing? Sorta?"

If she equivocates more Grace is just gonna call her on the bullshit. "Sorta," Grace says, and then it hits her. "Wait, so you can see him? So I'm not going crazy?"

A pitying look breaks across Heather's face, before it settles into something approaching sadness. "Everyone always thinks they're crazy instead of something else," she says, her voice wistful. "No, you're not crazy, there's an actual ghost in here, he seems pretty tame, I think."

"He exploded a lightbulb at me," Grace points out.

Again, Heather flaps her hand at her. "That's normal. That's like the most normal thing ever for ghosts. They have pressure issues." And the way she talks about it, it sounds like keeping a pet, or keeping a small child.

Without even a whisper, the ghost appears next to her, and it's only the last week that enables Grace to not flinch back in shock. He opens his mouth, lips moving rapidly, but nothing comes out, staring hard at Heather.

Heather straightens, looking at Grace with a profoundly confused look on her face. "Did he just show up?"

The confirmation that she's not so much going insane makes her weak at her knees. "Yes, yes he did."

"Ah," Heather says, matter of fact, then, "um."

The ghost crosses his arms, and this time she can even see the faint folds in his shirt, where before she could only make out the vague form of clothing over him.

Heather stares blankly at Grace for a few too long moments, blinking rapidly, as if the blinking will somehow make it so she can think faster.

Somehow, it's the most awkward she's felt in a while.

"So you can tell?" Grace ventures, once the silence becomes a bit too much.

Heather slowly nods, her eyes unfocusing.

The Ghost stares Heather down, unblinking, unmoving, as if he has become a block of solid ice.

"Um," Heather says again, and she slowly withdraws her hand from her messenger bag, and puts it up, defensive. "Uh, I really don't want to offend it. Him."

The ghost doesn't move, still doing his best impersonation of a statue.

Out of impulse, something strange, Grace puts her hand out to his shoulder and...it's not quite like something solid, but there's some resistance before her hand passes through him, and he jerks back, flickering out, like a computer simulation glitching out, and he disappears again.

The second he's gone, Heather relaxes, like a balloon letting out its air. "Oh thank god," she mutters, resting her head on the back of the overstuffed chair. "Oh thank god that was too intense."

"Sorry?" Grace says.

Heather shakes her head, squeezing her eyes shut. "Is there a burger place nearby? I could use a burger."

5

G race takes her to the nearest hole-in-the-wall Greek burger joint and Heather orders way more food than a normal person, and they squeeze into a plastic-lined booth. Heather looks torn up and exhausted, and Grace feels somewhat bemused and normal.

After the disinterested waiter drops off the burgers and Heather takes several large bites, she waves her hand, as if clearing the air. "So, you have a ghost, he's been there for a while, and I think he'd react negatively to trying to get him to go away," she blurts out, and then takes a large slurp of a milkshake. "He was tame, until he showed up and I had my hand around some charms."

Still feeling like this is all unreal, Grace shrugs. "You can just tell that?"

She nods, then shakes her head, then nods again. "Sorta." Taking a big bite of the burger, she chews thoughtfully. "He wasn't openly malicious. So that's good."

"He did explode the lightbulb."

"And that was probably unintentional."

"Didn't look unintentional. He was annoyed by me," Grace says, in memory of the blank stare and the angry blinking. "I don't know if he liked me up on the ladder."

Heather shrugs, too casual, then takes a beaten up pad of paper out of her messenger bag and puts it on the table between them. "Okay. Let's establish a timeline," she says, twirling a chewed up pencil in between her hands. "Did you see the ghost before you purchased the place?"

Grace shakes her head, a bit amused at the sudden official nature of the questioning.

"How close to buying it did you see the ghost?" Heather scribbles a few things in her notebook, then flips it around.

She sketches out an actual timeline, as if this is a thing she's done so many times she needs a template for it.

"The first night I stayed there," Grace says, absentmindedly. "But it wasn't actually, you know, a full ghost thing. It was more of just a bit of creepy movement. Like a shadow woke me up."

Heather makes a few marks in the notebook. "So he started materializing when you spent time there," she says, still not quite making eye contact. "Did you say anything to him?"

"I thought a hobo had come in, so I asked who was there." For some reason, Grace feels like she has done something wrong, stumbled over some transgression, handled the situation poorly. It's a feeling she has a lot, and it's not a welcome one.

Heather shrugs. "I'm guessing he vanished then?"

She nods.

"Sounds about right," she says, wistful. "Generally spirits are uneasy when they're first spoken to."

"But now I talk to him all the time, is that okay?" Grace blurts out.

"Oh totally. Just catches them by surprise, ya know?"

Grace didn't know, so she says nothing, the feeling of doing wrong piling up in her stomach and making the burger in front of her seem like the worst thing ever, a pile of grease.

"When was the first time you saw any details? Of, you know, his face and stuff?" Heather asks, twirling the pen absentmindedly.

Grace tries to look anywhere but at the food on the table. "A few nights later," she says, suddenly feeling like there's a lump in her throat, making it difficult to swallow or speak. "I think I surprised him, I got close, he...sorta touched me?"

Heather blinks at her, but doesn't directly meet her eyes. "So you can feel him?" Her voice is smoothly nonjudgemental, but Grace still gets the feeling crawling over her.

"Only sorta. It's not...not..."

Heather nods again, writes a few things down, and Grace peers over her shoulder to read it, but it looks like shorthand. As if sensing her gaze, Heather flips the notebook shut.

"Well, I can't say for certain, but it seems like he's a normal displaced spirit," Heather says, twisting one of the scarves between her fingers. "Seems tame, mostly tame, some spooky shit unless you piss them off."

"Piss them off?" Cause that didn't sound fun. "How do I get him to leave?"

This time Heather finally meets her eyes, startled. "You don't, not really," she says, voice dipping into disgusted. "They're the ones stuck there, not you."

"But it's my house, I bought it," Grace shoots back, the pool of horror growing into her stomach. "He could've hurt me. I was on a ladder and he exploded glass."

Heather throws up her hands, over dramatic. "And he's a ghost, he doesn't much have a way of measuring how much pressure he puts on fragile items!" She screws her face up, as if suddenly aware of how loud she is. "I mean, unless he actually harms you, intentionally harms you, you shouldn't do anything."

"Can he actually harm me?" Grace asks, tucking her hands underneath her to resist the urge to shrink back into herself.

Heather looks caught in a lie, eyes wide, looking anywhere but at her. "It's...possible. But unlikely," she rushes to say. "It's rare, for them to appear enough to be able to harm like anything serious. Most just...eventually fade away."

"How long does that take?"

Heather twists her face again. "It varies," she says, soft. "Some never do. Some do after they get laid to rest. Some do just...just because." She clears her throat again. "Do you have any idea how old he is?"

Grace shakes her head. "He'll mouth stuff at me, but I can't read lips in English," she says, hunching in on herself.

Heather's eyebrows draw up, and she starts to eat her burger again, before shrugging it off. "There are some things you can do to be able to hear him," she says thoughtfully. "Or at least speed it along. It'll probably happen naturally with you, the more time you spend in there."

That sounds ominous to Grace, but everything sounds ominous to her. "Just me, though?"

Heather blinks lazily, seemingly much more invested in the food than the conversation, a sharp departure from before. "Usually just the people that spend the most time in the location, that's how it works." She flips open the pad of paper again to a different page, scribbles down an email address and rips out the page and gives it to Grace. "Can you, I dunno, email me with updates? I usually don't see ghosts this early in the process, it's cool."

"Uh, sure?" Grace takes it, sticking it in her pocket, still feeling like she's done a ton of things wrong. "But, um, what do I do? Now?"

"Chat with him," Heather says, casual. "The more you involve him, the stronger he will be."

"That's ominous."

"It is what it is. Or sell your house, those are the options," Heather says, her eyes scanning the crowd, but lazily, like she more wants to avoid eye contact than looking for someone.

"Going back, how would he hurt me?"

She shrugs again, and Grace is acutely aware that Heather doesn't actually care about her, just about the ghost and the interesting case.

WHEN GRACE ROLLS up the interior door, the ghost is waiting for her, his arms crossed and his eyebrows drawn.

She stills, the second she's inside, and locks eyes with him.

The corners of his mouth tug down into a proper scowl, and he blinks at her, slow and deliberate.

"Are you trying to do Morse code at me now?" She asks, setting down her purse and rolling back the door. "Cause I don't understand it."

He rolls his eyes, and follows her as she trails her way through the warehouse, making note of how the drywall looks in the light of the setting sun.

"You're the one that exploded the lightbulb, I'm just trying to make sure I'm safe," Grace says, idle, running her hand over the screws she put in that morning.

This wall, the low wall, she would eventually build up to be a wall of bookcases, the cubed kind that are kinda sorta in fashion but kinda sorta considered kitschy, but Grace loves them.

She trails her fingers along the edge of it, her mind absently falling to orders and angles and the places she would need to go to make it happen, and...

She notices the ghost trailing his hand right where she had trailed hers.

She snaps her head over to him, and he jerks his head up, looking for all the world guilty.

"What are you doing?" She asks, her voice going very calm, exactly the way it used to go reflexively when Rey did something bad, and she hates it. She hates that her very voice betrays her and goes right into her bad instincts the moment she's scared.

He mouths something at her, then scowls in obvious frustration, opening his arms wide in a helpless movement.

She squints at him, and he squints back. "The psychic--" he pulls a face at the mention of her-- "the psychic said you were getting stronger? By me being here?"

Relief crowds his face and he nods enthusiastically.

"Is that what you're doing? Getting stronger?"

As if sensing a trap, he nods, more tentative this time.

"From me?" She can feel something approaching panic start to grow up inside of her, rushing at her stomach and squeezing at her lungs. "Are you taking energy from me?"

He watches her, an eyebrow raised, before see-sawing with his hand. He nods, then shakes his head, scowling at the frustration of their inability to communicate.

It feeds into the panic, just a bit, and she jerks further away from him.

His eyebrows snap up at her reaction, and he takes a step back, hands up.

Cause Rey would call it this all the time. Said she was his recharge. Said he could take and take and take from her, cause all she had to do was exist and be there for him when he got back from whatever the hell illegal thing he was doing at that time. Said that every little motion with her, every little time he laid his hands on her, said he got something from her.

He had even called her his supply, once, and then him and his friends had laughed about it.

She knows, now, that all of his statements, all of his cruelty, was textbook narcissism, but, but...

But now she's huddled in a corner next to an unfinished wall, her hands around her head like she's some little child, and...

And the ghost is crouched near her. Not too near, but just enough so that the first thing she sees when she opens her eyes and comes back into the world of the present and not in the tumultuous past, is his face, looking way more spooked than he has any right to be.

They lock eyes, cause that seems to be the only thing they do, before he sits back, eyebrows up, wrapping his own arms around his knees and sitting just as much like a child as she feels right now.

She drops her arms away from her head, because she is reflexively acting like she is a child who could be beaten in front of a creature that can't technically touch anything. Breathing hard, she tries to push herself up from the corner, but her arms are shaking too much, so she sits, blinking hard at the chair in the corner so she doesn't have to look at the questioning face in front of her.

So she jerks when, in a touch of freezing cold, he reaches to her, his hand hovering over her arm, as if he is attempting to help her up.

His face twists in the familiar expression of frustration, before he smoothes it over, as if he was schooling his appearance for her alone.

"You don't have to do that," she says, and her voice trembles, because of course it's beyond her control. "The face...thing..." she gestures at her own, a bit inarticulate. "I got it, I'm weird, you're confused."

He narrows his eyes at her, but with a hint of a smile behind them.

She pushes herself up again, her arms working properly this time, and he remains close, the hand hovering over her arm, not quite touching, and the immediate post-panic attack prickliness starts to crawl in.

She turns away, striding to her makeshift kitchen and the too-large fridge that she had delivered, grabs an ice cream bar, and flops herself onto one of her very nice couches to munch on it.

She wishes she could say it has been years since she had a panic attack that bad, but she really can't. It has, at the most, been maybe two months, and the feeling of failing to get better claws at her throat.

As if completely unaware of what to do, the ghost hovers behind the couch, his face pinched.

"It was just a panic attack," she says, too loud, as if she can control what happened by pitching her voice up. "It happens, it's not a big deal."

Instead of walking around the couch, the ghost just vapors through it so he can stand in front of her, a clearly frustrated look on his face.

It doesn't help.

~

THE NEXT DAY she calls and invites her sister Deborah over to a proper dinner because she has a table now. And she doesn't want her sister to know how much she's trying to avoid a panic attack, but that's not really applicable. Really.

The moment she rolls up the interior door to let Deborah in, Deborah's eyebrows shoot up, but in an impressed way, not the skeptical way she did before.

"Oh, hey, this place looks great," she says, steel in her voice and a lightness in her step. "Did you do that wiring?"

Grace nods, a quick feeling of lightness bursting inside of her. "There's more to do, but hey, it looks like a place."

"It looks a lot like a place." Deborah puts a hand on the industrial stove, soft, as if she's actually impressed by her sister's work. "Everything works?"

The ghost appears, in the corner, standing next to the chair. He doesn't approach, but watches with a neutral look on his face. As if he's inherently skeptical, but not to the point of doing anything.

He locks eyes with Grace for a brief second, before nodding. He's touching the fabric of the chair again, almost a nervous tick. Whenever he's not actively following behind her, or interacting with her, he's touching the chair.

Deborah twirls around the wide open space, then flopping on the couches. "Oh my god, who'd you have to blow to get a couch this nice?" She lolls her head over, giving her sister a smile, as if that will soften the blow of such a callous statement.

"I saved money by getting this place for very little," Grace says, picking up a spatula and starting to make grilled cheese sandwiches. Grilled cheese sandwiches, wine, and ice cream for dessert. Just like they'd have when they were children, you know, minus the wine.

Deborah springs up from the couch, and paces around to the still unfinished wall. "Are you going to do that cube thing? The bookcase thing like the ones from Ikea?"

"I am absolutely not getting any furniture from Ikea." Grace wags the spatula at her. "I am getting it from a friend who's a respected designer who's giving me a discount because I saved his renovation from getting flooded a year ago. Ikea. Seriously."

Deborah shrugs, looking at the drywall. "But this wall wasn't there last time I was here, right? Or am I crazy."

The ghost watches her touch the drywall, the neutral look on his face shifting for a split second, before it returns.

"Yeah, I put that up. It's gonna be the work space on that side, so I can take clients without them, you know, being in my kitchen." She keeps a dual eye on her sister and on the ghost.

Her sister flops onto the overstuffed chair, shivers, then pops back up. "I think you have some drafts?"

"Yeah, there's something weird with the vents, I'm looking into it," Grace says, and the ghost has the actual audacity to wink at her. She wrinkles her nose back, and he smiles, wide.

As her sister paces around and explores the area, Grace throws herself into the cooking, the repetitive soothing motions lovely.

Her sister pauses, looking up at the wrought iron lighting fixture, still missing a lightbulb. Well, not missing, but shattered at the base. "Did you put that up like that?"

"No, I miscalculated the voltage and it exploded a bulb. It happens."

The ghost gives her a sharp look, but not an angry look. More like a look that's shocked into disbelieving, one that feels almost grateful, like she's understood something.

She shrugs at him cause what the hell else is she supposed to say.

"Mom's gonna flip when she sees this," Deborah says, wistful. "When you can bring her, someday, she's gonna be so proud."

"Maybe I'll just show her pictures. Not tell her the address or anything. Show her a pic of a different outside warehouse."

The ghost's eyebrows draw up, and with a smidgen of horror she realizes that he probably has no context to anything, and she really doesn't want to explain her horrible ex to a ghost.

Deborah shrugs, then climbed the spiral staircase to her little bedroom. Which is strewn with clothes cause she's unsatisfied with her current chest of drawers.

"Wow, this looks actually nice up here," Deborah calls back, leaning over the metal railing. "You really can see everything." She disappears from the railing, and a muffled flopping noise is the only indication that she probably jumped right on Grace's bed, and the exaggerated groan makes Grace smile.

"Food is coming up, don't get too comfy."

Deborah clatters down the spiral staircase, truly noisy, before taking her the plates and the bottle of wine to the table. "I can't believe you got a long table when you're so alone in here," she says. "This is a 'host the family for Thanksgiving' sort of table."

"And wouldn't that be nice," Grace mutters.

'Well, sure, but not gonna happen. Have you even had anyone else over? Anyone who, you know, knows you?" Her voice suddenly transitions into biting.

Grace blinks, and they start into their food on that strange note. "Not who know me, just...you know. Delivery people. A contractor or two."

Deborah raises her eyebrow, and takes it on herself to give her sister a very large pour of wine. "Well," she starts, then pauses, in the most anxiety inducing way possible. "Well, some of his...friends...reached out to mom."

The pit falls out of Grace's stomach. "Friends," she echoes.

"Yeah. She told them you were at the shithole apartment. They went there, and couldn't find you." Deborah takes a large gulp from the wine, as if to ease her own guilt for telling such a thing. "So mom at least knows you moved and didn't tell her."

The sandwich looks horrific on her plate, but Grace forces herself to take a bite, then another, then another. "And I bet she's hurt."

"Oh majorly," Deborah says, quick. "Doesn't understand why you wouldn't want her to know, or want his friends to know."

Out of the corner of her eye, she sees the ghost drift closer, peering at her, like he's trying to figure out what the fuck they're talking about. Which, granted, is not the most obvious of situations.

"Well, that's exactly why. That right there," Grace says, her mouth feeling dry but not wanting to reach for the wine. "Thanks for...why the hell are they looking for me now?"

Deborah shrugs, bewildered as well. "I mean, it doesn't make sense. It's been, what, a year and a half? Two years?"

"A year and four months," Grace says, without thinking. Cause she doesn't even have to think about that, there's just the number in the back of her head, letting her know exactly how much time has passed, exactly how much time since she slept in the truck, and exactly how much time since Rey got placed in prison.

"Right," Deborah says, drinking more again. "But. So you know."

Grace nods into her grilled cheese. "Yeah."

DEBORAH DRINKS SO much wine she crashes on the too large couch, leaving her older sister to throw a blanket over her and make sure she has water on the little table next to it.

The ghost solemnly watches her, then trails after her, climbing the stairs with her, as if he is unable to get up to the loft without them.

"I know, I know," Grace whispers at him, only okay with doing so because her sister is audibly snoring downstairs. "Can I just...explain later?"

Her own glass of wine still sits at the table, completely untouched.

The ghost nods, his eyebrows still drawn together, and he sits on the floor in the loft, so obviously troubled.

"I'm fine, I just don't want to talk too much cause my sister will wake up and want to know why I'm crazy and talking to myself," she says, though his obvious concern is almost...touching. Or soothing.

Though, really, she might be just projecting. He could be upset about any number of things, confused over what the hell is going on in his little world, many things. It might have nothing to do with her, only coincidental that she is in his space while it's happening.

As if sensing her thoughts, he extends his hand to her, small.

She impulsively reaches down and grasps his hand.

Or tries.

There's the moment of resistance, the moment where it seems like he is solid, before her hand moves through his.

He drops his hand, resting his chin on his knees, eyes sad.

She flops into her bed, still wearing all her clothes. "Please don't make me feel bad for having a bad ex," she whispers, squeezing her eyes shut.

Of course, there's no reply, so she presses the heels of her hands into her eyes and turns over, burrowing into her expensive coverlet.

THE NEXT MORNING, after bidding her very hungover little sister good-bye, she makes her way to her current design renovation, meeting a too enthusiastic Trixie there.

Trixie takes one look at her and smiles, huge. "We might've actually gotten some clearance to get some old style theater gobos in here," she says, in lieu of a greeting.

"That's gonna throw some weird shadows into some corners," Grace immediately says, speaking the first problem that comes into her mind, cause of course she does.

"And that's the fun part, we can figure out how to avoid that." Trixie is a never ending source of positivity, one that can bend and warp Grace's ability to deal.

They enter the house, and the owner already has a variety of gobos and lighting equipment strewn around, but is nowhere in sight, leaving the two relatively short girls with the ladder to hang them.

"Why gobos, though?" Grace asks, idle, setting up the ladder and making sure it doesn't slip.

"I think this room is gonna be a holiday room." Cause of course they work for people who can afford to have a separate room decorated just for holidays. "He mentioned he wanted it to look like it's snowing in the winter, and he wants ghosts around Halloween."

"He can literally drive two hours up the mountains, he'll get snow there," Grace grumps, but holds the ladder as Trixie gets into rigging. "This is...ridiculous."

"I know," Trixie breathes, "I love it."

They get all into their safety materials, then start hanging theater style lights. Which, you know, is fairly enjoyable, but hard work.

"How's that new place of yours?" Trixie asks, way too casual, and the hairs on the back of Grace's arms rise.

"I laid some drywall a few days ago, gonna make one of those cubed storage walls you see everywhere, thirteen feet tall." Grace says, cause that's harmless enough. Doesn't give any determining information, all that jazz.

Trixie gives her a quick glance before returning to tightening the screws on the light. "All by yourself?"

Grace shrugs and nods, before handing her a few gels to slot in front of the light.

"I knew you were a builder, but isn't that rough?" Trixie asks, slotting in the gel and switching on the gobo. Fake, all white ghosts fill the room, and the gobo makes them rise and fall across the walls.

Squashing a bit of laughter at the weirdness, Grace merely smiles instead. "I have time, no real deadline, get to do it right," she says, knowing that Trixie would respond to it. "Moderate budget, get to do it on my own time, on my own space, to my own specifications."

Trixie gives the aura that if she had time and free hands, she'd be clapping with joy, but instead she settles for giving Grace a brilliant smile. "That's the dream, I tell you," she says, wistful. "Tell me when you get to light it, I'll come over and help?"

Grace nods, squashing the immediate terror of the thought, watching the fake ghosts rise and fall on the wall. "Well, that area is window lit, mostly. Gonna do my drafting in there."

"Jesus Christ," Trixie says, jealousy dripping down her words. "How the fuck..." A gel pops, and they both stare at it again, before they both sigh, in unison.

"Great," Grace mumbles, and they begin to unscrew the gobo again.

"Seriously." Trixie joins in, and this is why they work well together.

~

LATER, as they load up their safety equipment into their cars, Trixie takes a deep breath and squares off at Grace.

"Hey," she says, and her tone of voice pools dread at the bottom of Grace's stomach. "Some guys came by the old office in Moorpark, asked about you."

Grace closes her eyes, because of course someone went by her old office. "Yeah, people do that."

Trixie's perfectly curated eyebrows draw up. "They were creepy," she says, definitive. "I said you moved to Maine and took their card instead of giving out your number." She pauses, before soldiering on. "I don't think they were customers, or else I'd give your email, but yeah."

"Yeah," Grace echoes, putting her toolkit into the back of her truck, before closing the lid down. "Look, if you could...not tell them where I am or anything..."

"No shit," Trixie snaps. "They were large men who asked why you haven't been to your old apartment in months, I wasn't gonna tell them anything."

And then there is the pause. The pause that always happens when something like this occurs to Grace. The pause where the other person sees something weird, and waits for Grace to explain it, to either confirm or deny their beliefs, to assuage their guilt for not knowing before.

It's an awful pause, one that some people barrel through, some people wait it out, and some people assume the worst.

So Grace just plasters on a smile. "Bad Ex, you know?" she says. "Sends friends like flying monkeys."

"Flying...monkeys?"

"You know, like Wizard of Oz? Flying monkeys? Come after you and try to bring you in?" Grace imitates the flapping of the wings. "Flying Monkeys."

"Riiiiight," Trixie says, drawing it out to at least four syllables. "Are you...safe?"

Grace shrugs, too loose, and she's fully aware it's not convincing at all. "I moved cities, but still work here. He'd have to trail me to find where I live, and I paint my truck every few months." She's immediately aware that it's too much information to give to a casual work friend, albeit one who she works very well with. "You don't have to worry."

"That's not a reassuring statement," Trixie says, but she tosses her perfect blond hair over her shoulders. "Well, good on you for getting out, call me if you need backup."

The idea of the pencil thin Trixie with her perfect hair and her work slacks standing up to Rey makes Grace smile. And, right on cue to get her out of the uncomfortable conversation, her phone rings.

She nods at Trixie, who gets into her own tiny car and pulls out. Shifting so she's comfortable in the cab of her truck, she answers, putting it on speaker phone.

"Reddy Designs," she says, resting her hands on the steering wheel for a split second, before turning the car on.

"Um," says the voice on the other end, and it's a vaguely familiar female voice. "Um, is this Grace? This is Heather. We spoke. About your...house issue."

After the conversation she just had, Grace almost jumps, her brain almost squeaking as it jumps gears. "Right, yes. What's up?"

"I think I got some more information for you, can we meet?"

And only after the last conversation does her heart jump. "How about at that burger place?"

"Yeah. That works." And the phone clicks off, leaving Grace with a puzzling lack of context.

～

GRACE TURNS onto the easy access street of the burger joint, parking the car with a wary look to the lot inhabitants.

No one spares her a glance, which is good, despite the creepy crawly feeling that she's being watched.

Once inside, Heather waves her over, still wearing too many scarves and trendy of clothing. "So I analyzed all the readings I did," she starts, before Grace is fully sitting down.

"You did readings?" Grace asks, her eyebrows drawing together. Heather hadn't done anything, just kept her hand in her messenger bag and her eyes up and looking around.

"I had sensors going, I'm not stupid," Heather says, defensive.

The waitress brings over milkshakes, and they sit in the plastic booths for a second, each enjoying them, before Heather very visibly shakes herself loose. "But yes. Readings. They're interesting." She pulls out the same pad of paper. "I'm about eighty percent sure he died in that corner, where you put the chair."

And the shift of thinking of her ghost as dead hits her like a brick, even though she knows and she knew that to be a ghost he must've already passed. "Oh," she says, dumb. "Should I move the chair?"

Heather shrugs.

"Okay." Grace takes a deep breath. "Right. Someone died in my house."

"And never left." Heather flips to a page, and all of the buying and selling details of the warehouse are there, written in cramped and crooked penmanship.

Details that Grace knows well. First built in 1929, then converted and switched hands all throughout the Great Depression, before finally being renovated during the 1950s to the bakery.

"I cross checked these dates, and the building was sold in 1932 after the death of a worker, Rodrick Michaelson." She flips a page, and...she had glued a picture, clearly printed from the internet, of her ghost.

Well, probably the ghost. It's a fuzzy picture, one of the stereotypes of an old timey picture, obviously cut from a group photo of all the warehouse workers.

But the cut of the jawline and the crook of the nose is all her ghost.

"Rodrick. Huh." Grace tilts her head, still focusing on the picture. "Huh."

"Is that him?" Heather asks, eager. "Cause there's one other death in the building but I think that's him."

"I think so...another death?"

"That one was of old age, and those don't really leave traditional ghosts, you know?" Heather bounces in her seat, jabbing a finger at the picture of the ghost. "But that's him?"

Grace peers at it closer. "I mean it's fuzzy, but I think that looks like him. It has the jawline."

Heather smiles, wide and brilliant, eyes more alight than Grace thought possible on such a hipster girl. "I thought so," she breathes. "He died when a piece of machinery exploded and he got shrapnel to the chest. Have you seen his chest? Without a shirt?"

Grace levels her with a look, but Heather seems completely unaware of how weird of a question that is. "No? I just got to where I saw details of his clothing at all."

"Right. Right. Has he done anything else? Anything interesting?"

Besides give her a panic attack, not really.

"He walks behind me a lot, and says he's getting energy from me," Grace says, forcing the words past the odd amalgamation of shame and pride about the incident.

"You can talk to him now?" She all but squeals.

Grace shakes her head, and Heather's face falls. "I asked if that was what he was doing, and he nodded."

"That's less cool than talking to him." Heather points out. "Though...good. I guess. If he's communicating."

It all feels surreal, like to Heather she's some neat discovery, and not, you know, living with a dead person as a roommate. "He seems sad, a lot."

Heather just shrugs, as if that's not a factor at all. "I mean, most ghosts are sad. That's why they're ghosts. I think." It seems to refocus her, and she flips to another page in her notebook. "So he's not the most powerful that's ever been recorded, but I think that because you actually, you know, live there, he has the potential to be pretty damn exciting."

Exciting is an ominous word, but Grace keeps that to herself. "So what should I do?"

"Unless he threatens you--"

"—Like the lightbulb--"

"You should be fine, though it may be strange. If you start seeing thunderbolts inside, I'd consider moving." Heather smiles, like it's a joke.

"Thunderbolts, got it," Grace replies dryly. "Any indoor weather, I'll leave."

"Especially if it strikes you. Electric feedback is one of the most predictable anger responses in ghosts like this, especially with the violent death thing." She pokes her finger at the cause of death in her notebook. "Like how the lights flicker when they're confused. Electricity and ghosts is weird."

"So would extra grounding of the cables be good?" Grace asks, trying to not look at the cause of death and instead force the conversation into things she can do.

Heather blinks at her, rapidly, before shrugging. "I don't know?"

∾

SHE STOPS at Home Depot on the way home and buys a grounded lamp and some extra cable cords to get everything squared away.

By the time she pulls up to the house, though, the pleasantly sunny autumn day is clouded over, and the smell of city rain is in the back of her throat, and after all the talk of thunderbolts and electricity, she is not in the mood.

But she leaves her truck outside, not wanting to deal with the mud on her floor, and the moment she rolls up the interior door her ghost is on the other side of it, eyebrows drawn up in a parody of concern.

"I was at work, relax," she mutters, putting down her bags of construction stuff and the lamp. "Rodrick."

The name strikes him like a slap, and he recoils away.

She straightens, looking at him. "That's your name, right?"

He seems to gather himself, and he leans in, close to her personal space, eyes narrowed. Then, after a second, he nods.

"The psychic who was here, the one with the scarves, she did some research on the building," Grace says, partially so she can say something and partially to stop him from giving her that look. "She says you were either Rodrick, or some old guy who died in his sleep during a nap."

The ghost rolls his eyes, then holds up one finger: the first.

"So, Rodrick." Grace says, again, trying it out, rolling the name around her mouth like it's something to taste. "You've been here since 1932."

He hesitates, then nods, the troubled look returning to his face.

"The world has changed, hasn't it."

He rolls his eyes again, as if her very question is silly.

The small rush of confirming his name wears off abruptly. "She said you died in an explosion."

A narrowing of eyes, then a too casual shrug.

"That's it? A shrug?" She drags in the lamp over to where she wants to put her yet nonexistent desk, uncoiling the cord and plugging it into the bare extension cord. "I just confirmed that you died and that I'm not going crazy and I get a shrug?"

He gives her a look, the sort of look you give a particularly stupid small child.

"Is that why this place sold so much? You were haunting it?" She plugs in the lamp, and it shines true. None of the initial flickering that she's come to expect with this place.

Like a moth, Rodrick draws close to the lamp, and it's surreal. The light shines right through him, rendering him partially transparent.

Not that he's always opaque to her, but it further drives home the oddness.

"I talked to the psychic, she said ghosts have electrical issues, so I got a properly grounded lamp, you like it?"

Rodrick puts his hand through the lamp, and it doesn't even flicker. Turning his hand over and over in the middle of the light bulb, he smiles, slow.

"Yeah, I thought you might." Grace flops over into the overstuffed chair in his corner, and it truly is a comforting chair. "So you've just been here. For like 80 years."

He keeps on turning his hand over and over in the lamp, not paying her an inch of attention.

She studies him, studies the way the light streams through him, how the close cropped hairs on his head shine, how his otherworldly blue eyes glow.

He's handsome, somewhat, in that way that things that are unreal can be beautiful in how separate from reality they are.

"She said one day you'll be able to talk to me, and I'll be able to hear." Grace says, and his attention immediately snaps to her. "Said if I spend enough time, put enough energy into this space, I'll be able to hear when you speak. Or something like that."

He leaves the lamp, coming right up to her and leaning over her in the chair. She's not sure if he means it to be intimidating, but it's certainly interesting, with both of his hands firmly braced on the arms of the chair. If she hadn't, you know, been accustomed to Rey and all of his intimidation, large and small, she would've been scared, but as it is this is small potatoes.

"Has that happened with you yet?" She lifts her chin to look him in his otherworldly eyes.

He shakes his head.

"So you haven't been able to talk to someone for like eighty years."

Another shake of the head.

"Isn't that lonely?"

He stills, in only the way that someone who doesn't breath can still, just slowly blinking at her.

It's awkward, and awful, the stillness, and she's the one to read eye contact. "I guess that was insensitive of me?"

He nods, slow.

She sighs, and he leans back, just a little, now less into the intimidating space and more into the, you know, normal conversation space.

The chair is truly comfortable, and the chill isn't even bothering her at the moment, though another throw blanket would have to be added for wintertime. She pulls her knees to her chest, curling up proper.

He stays, arms braced on the chair, expectant, as if waiting for her to say something, but she braces her head on her hand, mind blank for a few seconds.

"My ex sent people to look for me at my old office," she says, sudden, not sure why or if she should speak.

He raises an eyebrow.

"He's still in prison, but he sent them trying to find me anyways."

He tilts his head towards her couch, where her sister slept the night before.

"Yeah, that's what she was talking about. He's a bad one." She curls up tighter in the chair, relishing in the comfort and forcing the words past the instinct that she should never talk about this. "So, I guess, if anyone comes looking around this place, I dunno, let me know? Point to that spot on the wall the moment I come in if they do?"

His eyebrows draw up, but he nods.

"I've taken...precautions, they shouldn't be able to easily find this place, but...yeah. It's a different city, it's a horrible commute to my actual work, and I've never talked about buying some place before, so it'd be weird for them to guess, and I park my truck inside, and people know to not tell them anything, but yeah." She's rambling, but he can't really interrupt her, so she lets herself. "Last I heard he's not supposed to get out of prison for another year but I guess that could change, I'm trying to not keep track cause that...would be bad for me?"

He tilts his head, as if waiting for her to explain the thing he's really curious about. But, of course, she's probably just projecting. She's been told she does that.

So she wraps her arms around her legs, relishing in the small bit of physical pressure she gives herself, in that little bit of childish comfort. "They'd have to follow me from some place at my job, and I don't think they have the patience for that."

He opens and closes his mouth, but of course she hears nothing, and his face twists with frustration.

"It's stupid, it's fucked up, but that's...kinda how it is." She pushes herself up, all of a sudden wanting to move, to stretch her legs, even after the active day of hanging lights. "But I'm here, I'm able to work, and I'm safe. So that's good."

He stays put, eyes watching her, brows furrowed, and she wishes she could know if he's just confused or if he's judging her. For all she knows, being from the nineteen thirties, he could be thinking all horrible sort of thoughts and she's just projecting all of her issues onto him because he literally can't reply back.

"I can't go to the police, his buddies are on the force. The only reason he's in prison is cause he got caught in a federal thing."

He rolls his eyes, and she can't stand it anymore.

So she picks up her putty knife, getting to work with covering the screw heads in her partial wall. It's minor, but it's better to use the patch primer than to have it wobble later when she affixes the bookcase.

He watches her, brows furrowed, until she can't stand it anymore.

"Heather says you can cause thunderbolts while angry?"

His shoulder shake at that, as if he's laughing, but she can't see his face well enough to check.

"Yeah it sounded fake to me too."

6

The next morning, after rolling out of bed at a too late time and dressing in her rough work clothes to go hang more lights, Rodrick watches her a bit too closely, following her a bit too near, his frown a bit too thoughtful.

He watches as she scrambles some eggs, watches as she eats them with some coffee, and watches as she ties her black hair back into something resembling a braid.

It grates on the edges of her nerves, something approaching irritation but not quite there yet. It's the same feeling of something about to go sideways, of something about to leave her in a bad position, but she can't quite yet place her finger on it.

As she picks up her keys to open up the interior door, however, he slides in place in front of the padlock, giving her a hard look.

She stares at him, then at the keys in her hand. "Yes?"

He gives her truck a significant look, then shakes his head.

"Um, I do have to go to work," she says, flipping the keys in her hand.

He again shakes his head, a scowl appearing on his lips.

"No, I really do," she says, then makes a move for the lock.

He smoothly steps between her again, as if he, a dead specter with no actual body or physical mass, could block her.

Still, she stops. "Seriously, this is still a thing I have to do," she says, her voice sounding much smaller than she wants in her ears.

Rey would block her from going out all the fucking time, and the last thing she needs is the ghost that came with her new house trying to do the same.

The look on his face suddenly softens, and he extends his hand, letting it hover over her shoulder, as if wishing to touch her.

She squints at him. "I can't tell if you're trying to stop me from leaving or trying to comfort me?"

He nods, cause that's helpful.

"I'll be back," she says, sudden. "Me leaving for work doesn't mean I won't come back."

He scowls at her, but it's the embarrassed scowl of someone caught in something foolish.

She smiles at him, a little, and he softens a bit, his face smoothing over. "I'll be back later, it's probably not even a full day today, we're just doing light focus on a rich guy's home in Beverly Hills."

He reaches, his hand against her face, and she feels the faintest whisper of pressure, a faintest bit of actual substance against her.

She closes her eyes against the cold, but it's...not as bad. As before.

"I'll be okay," she says, soft. "I've been around for a while, and he's in prison, and I've been okay so far."

He gives her a critical glance, as if he doesn't believe a word she's saying.

"I mean, I clawed my way out to be able to buy this place, that has to count for something."

Reluctance bleeding into his every motion, he moves aside, letting her unlock the padlock and roll up the interior door.

Still, as she backs her truck out, she sees him watching and the lights flickering behind him.

～

FOCUSING LIGHTS IS, as always, fun but mindless work, and her and Trixie make short work of the tiny lighting grid they set up.

Afterwards, as they walk down the driveway to their cars, Trixie bars her with her arm, pulling Grace behind some bushes.

"You see that car?" Trixie whispers, pointing at a small sedan parked right behind her truck. "I think those guys I told you about are there. That's their car."

Instinctively, Grace grabs Trixie's arm, peering out between the trees.

In the tiny sedan sit four comically large men, idling the car right behind her truck, and Grace can't make out their faces or features, except for their size.

"How could you tell?"

Trixie points, sort of generically in their direction. "The big one in the driver's seat. The hair, it's...distinctive."

It's the high and tight cut that many of Rey's friends favored, that most of their political ilk preferred.

Her heart thudding, Grace counts to four, then faces Trixie. "Is your car around the back?"

Trixie nods, slow.

"Can you give me a ride for a bit?"

"Sure," she says, her voice a little high, and Grace gets a rush of sympathy for her. Grace, she's been followed and she's been intimidated and she's been threatened, but she has no reason to believe that little pretty California blonde has ever dealt with the sheer level of weirdness that she has.

Grace starts to walk towards where Trixie's car must be, but she tugs Trixie along, where Trixie seems to be rooted to the ground.

"Grace, are they dangerous?"

"Probably," Grace says, frank, not wanting to coddle her work friend at this very moment. "Probably not to you."

Trixie eyes her, disbelieving, before relenting and leaving their safe little shelter and striding with Grace to her sedan.

Grace doesn't look back to see if the men spot them, her skin crawling, like bugs up and down her spine and creeping along the back of her arms and dripping down her legs, and she wills herself to walk slowly, as if nothing is wrong.

Trixie throws open her car door, and Grace calmly sits down next, because nothing draws the eye faster than desperate motion.

The closed door rush of hot air hits her, and she takes a moment to breathe hard out of her nose, before turning to Trixie. "Can I crash on your couch tonight?"

"Yeah of course," Trixie says, her voice still high and strained. "I mean, yeah."

"I'll get an Uber and get my truck in the morning, at a weird time or something. They won't be here all night," she says, halfway reassuring Trixie and halfway forming the plan in her mind.

"Yeah." Trixie stares at the dashboard of her car, before starting the engine and smoothly pulling out of the spot.

The car is still idling behind Grace's truck, waiting. Grace watches it, until they turn down the street and lose sight.

She turns back to the front, feeling like her heart is pounding too hard and not hard enough for the situation. Like she should be panicking more, despite the fact that she feels she is panicking the perfect amount at the moment.

"The fuck?" Trixie whispers, giving her a sidelong look as she turns down the street. "Seriously, the fuck?"

Grace stares at the passing streetlights, not really wanting to answer the implicit question. "So..."

Trixie nods. "Yesssss?"

"So I have a bad ex."

"That's not bad ex shit, that's Irish mafia level shit."

Grace makes finger guns, because it's not the most wrong someone's ever been. "Yeah."

"So he stalks you at job sites with three of his biggest friends? That's not an ex, that's a serial killer."

"Oh, no, the ex is in prison. These are just his...lackeys?"

Trixie blinks wildly as she drives, and if it wasn't for the fact that Grace hasn't ever even heard of her crashing she'd be very scared right about now.

"Lackeys." Her voice is flatter than anything she's ever heard. "People don't have lackeys."

"Yeah well." Grace stares out the window again, cause looking at overpriced Beverly Hills houses is far better than thinking about the monumentally shitty decisions she's made in the past. "This is why I lived in that shithole for a year."

Trixie scowls out at the road, before merging smoothly onto the major road. "You've never...said anything?" She says, her voice small. "I mean, how long ago did you...you said he's an ex."

"I got away about a year and four months ago, if that's what you're asking," Grace snaps, then winces at the harshness.

"Yeah that," Trixie says, before falling silent. "I mean, We were working on that Calabasas project before that, and that Pasadena house, and like...many more."

"It didn't come up." Which, frankly, is a shitty excuse, and everyone always tells her it is, even that therapist she saw for a bit. "It didn't come up, and I was scared if it did." There she went into too honest territory. It's almost like she has to choose between blatantly incomplete answers or bitingly vulnerable ones.

Trixie is pale, and they don't speak for the rest of the ride.

SHE CRASHES on Trixie's modest couch, then leaves a note in the morning when she gets an Uber at 4 AM back to the Beverly Hills house.

Her truck, thankfully, is the only car still parked on the street, albeit with a parking ticket.

She stares at the yellow and pink strip of paper, before tossing it in the passenger's seat and starting her car. Her eyes hurt so bad they ache, and every time she blinks there's a new piece of rough sand in them.

"Jesus Christ," she mutters, before turning off her car and checking her tires, under the bumper, and lifting the hood.

No new equipment, so she heaves a deep breath, starting the car again, and driving out.

The drive halfway up the mountain takes a hell of a lot less time at 4 AM than it does during rush hour, the entire ride a surreal passing of street lamps and empty LA streets. Well, empty for LA, at least, which means that she saw at least twenty other cars.

And, as she pulls up to her warehouse up the hill, her eyes hurting, a sense of dread pools into her stomach, but it's nothing new. After a certain point, the dread in your stomach becomes common place, and you start to be able to forget it. It becomes part of you, a part that hates yourself and hates your situation and hates everything about yourself, but it's a part, almost as inseparable as your left foot.

Grace had put herself through a lot of therapy in order to draw it out of herself, bit by bit, only to have some jocks camped out behind her truck ruin all that hard work.

And she got a parking ticket.

Kicking open her truck door, she undoes the padlock on the outside doors, then rolls up the interior...to see Rodrick staring, almost where she left him, eyes wide.

The knot in her throat getting bigger, she rolls her truck inside, then closes up behind her.

He opens his mouth, as if to speak, then closes it before he even gets a chance to mouth anything at her, instead leveling her with a wounded look, as if she is the one who did everything wrong today.

"What." She snaps, slamming her truck door with a bit too much force and rolling down the door.

He narrows his eyes at her, then opens his arms up wide, as if to ask what right back.

Behind him, all the lights flicker at once, plunging them into pitch darkness for about two seconds before flipping back on.

She flinches, then immediately hates herself for that reaction, and turns on her heel and strides to her loft.

He follows after her, a cold presence at her back, a stormy look on his face. All lights but the grounded lamp flicker, in time with his steps, as if some sort of otherworldly and unnatural punctuation.

Of course he's unhappy. After that sappy talk and those sappy words and her reassurances that she'd be back...she didn't come back. And now it's almost 5AM and the sun will be rising in little under two hours and she...can't deal. Just can't. The ability to deal with whatever emotional storm her undead apparent roommate is brewing up is just...not possible.

"I crashed on a friend's couch, what do you want from me?" She turns, at the base of the spiral stairs, throwing her arms up. "I couldn't get home before now."

And if there's anyone she can tell why, the small ugly part in herself knows it would be Rodrick, for he couldn't tell anyone. It'd be just as a good as a secret, but that part of her now doesn't want to divulge. To keep it to herself, that she got spooked by some men in a tiny sedan and then could barely drive home.

He flinches back from her, the lights swinging and flickering.

"And while I'd love, I'd just love to rehash all the things about my shitty day, I haven't really slept yet, and my fucking eyes hurt."

Lightning fast, so fast he might've well teleported, he's in front of her, on the first step, leaning down so he's nose to nose.

She jumps, her heart pounding.

He narrows his unreal blue eyes thinner, locking eyes, as if he thinks he can control her by his own thoughts. Keep her pinned down in one place until he gets answers.

Answers that, known shitty coping mechanisms aside, he isn't gonna get right now.

"Oh stop that," she mutters, pushing past him, feeling the strange almost there pressure of him, before she moves through him and climbing the stairs.

A lightbulb on the other side of the warehouse pops, then explodes, and she flinches at the sound of tinkling glass.

"Can you stop that?" She says. Her eyes hurt. Everything hurts. Her head hurts, her back hurts, everything.

He opens his arms wide again, an even bigger picture of frustration.

"I was followed, okay?" She half yells at him, stopping in the middle of the staircase. "Someone tried to follow me home from work, so I crashed with a friend! It's not the end of the world!"

Sudden, the lights plunge them into darkness, and she takes a deep, heaving breath, then another, then another.

Slowly, one at a time, the lights flicker back on, starting with the far corner and slowly, slowly reaching them, and she just looks at him.

He's transparent, more transparent than before, his eyes wide and stricken, but his clothes vague and his hair mostly a blur above his head.

She hugs herself, sudden, the shame a growing maw within her. And they stare at each other, for a few seconds, before...something in his posture, something in the way he stands, seems to relent. He stands down.

She nods, and he nods back, and she turns and slowly resumes her walk up the spiral staircase, flopping directly into her bed, not even bother changing her clothes.

~

WHEN DAWN BREAKS, she half wakes to the feeling of pressure on the bed, and the half sound of whispers in the air.

She stirs, but sleep draws her back down into it, sinking its claws and pulling her down.

~

SHE SPENDS the next day tiredly puttering around the internet with some furniture and lighting designs, never fully feeling like she's awake.

A little after noon, her phone rings, and thank god it's Trixie.

"Hello?"

"I got your note, did you even make it back to your car okay?" Trixie's voice is muffled, the muffling of using speakerphone in a car.

Grace clicks out of a lighting catalogue and onto a furniture one. "Yeah they were gone when I got to the car."

There's a pause, and Grace gets the horrid feeling that Trixie is concerned but doesn't exactly want to say it, and the moment over the phone drags on.

Out of the corner of her eye, she sees Rodrick appear mid action, mid step of pacing around.

After a long second, Trixie blows out a long exhale. "Do you need a ride anywhere? Need to rent a car?"

Grace shakes her head, then immediately feels silly. "I'm not on the site until Monday, I'll think of something."

"Fucking fine," Trixie all but grumbles. "Call me if you, you know."

"Yeah."

The phone clicks off, and Grace knows, she just knows, she should've said more and should've given more, but...she feels like she just has no more to give.

After a split second, Rodrick's attention turns to her, and he strides over and jabs his finger at the phone.

She gives him a blank look, fully realizing that she does not have the ability to deal with the guessing game right now. "What."

He jabs at the phone again, drawing his eyebrows up.

"It's...a phone. Oh." She blinks at him. "They didn't have these in the 1930s, not like this, right?"

He shakes his head.

"That was my friend calling to check up on me, cause I left before she woke up."

He nods, slow, as if almost getting it.

"Seriously, have you never seen a cell phone before?"

He shakes his head, then mimes her texting on it.

"Yeah, I can send messages, but also talk? It does...a lot of things?"

He narrows his eyes, but it's not the angry look, more like an inherently skeptical look, and she gets an idea.

"You've seen me use this, right?" She gestures at her laptop, then opens up a word document. At his nod, she shows him the keyboard.

"Point at the letters, I'll type them and you can say something to me."

He jerks his head to her, then back down at the keyboard, then back up at her.

"Seriously. It's like those ouija boards." At his lack of response, she sighs. "Never mind, just..."

She trails off as he jabs his finger almost into the keyboard at a letter, than another, then another.

"Jeez," she mutters as she types. "Should'a tried this one a bit sooner."

He gives her a quelling look, then leans down so he's on her level and can see the screen.

WHY DID YOU BUY THIS PLACE?

She blinks at the question, cause for everything she's chattered at him about, she never thought he'd actually have that as something he was curious about.

"I mean, I wanted a space to set up a workshop? And a place to live?"

He rolls his eyes then starts jabbing his finger again.

WHY NOT YOUR SISTER?

She mouths the words as she types.

"You mean why not just live with her?" At his nod, she shrugs. "Rey knows where she lives."

He mouths 'Rey' at her, wrinkling his nose.

WHY IS HE IN PRISON?

She stares at the screen, breathing hard through her nose. "Cause he got caught with tax fraud in three states. Nothing to do with me."

He gives her the most unimpressed look, then stares at the keyboard, as if at a loss.

Grace sits back, stretching out that one point between her shoulders that always freezes up when she sleeps on a couch, letting him ponder the keyboard and probably the only way to communicate that he's had in 80 some odd years.

Instead she lets her eyes wander, back to the half wall and the wooden shelves she wants to put up, and her woodcutting equipment she should really get out of storage, and doesn't really think of anything until Rodrick's frantically waving in her face, a frown on his lips.

Once he gets her attention he gives her a quelling look, then starts poking at the computer keys again.

WHY THE PSYCHIC

"You exploded a lightbulb at me, how was I supposed to know you weren't going to hurt me?"

He throws up his hands again, then back at the keyboard.

I CAN'T TOUCH ANYTHING HOW CAN I HURT ANYTHING?

"Broken glass can hurt!" She says, indignant. "And I didn't know, that, then."

He nods, as if that makes sense, then he points at the wall.

HOW MUCH ARE YOU BUILDING

She throws a glance at it. "Well, I'm gonna sector that part out by a partial wall, so I have space to work that's not, you know, directly where I live." She pauses, something occurring to her. "Is that okay with you?"

He equivocates, then nods, tapping at the keys again.

I THINK SO?

After a pause of staring at her, as if trying to place his words, he resumes.

THERE HASN'T BEEN CHANGE HERE IN A LONG TIME.

And she supposes that's true, as frustrating as that sounds. "Well, uh, we will figure out a way for you to tell me if you hate something? Besides exploding lightbulbs?" She throws a glance at the one that exploded the night before with a pointed look.

He visibly sighs, so much she can swear she can hear him.

ACCIDENT.

"Sure," she quips. "Just like the one with the ladder was an accident."

He gives her a narrowed eyed look, then stares at the keys again, as if stymied.

"I mean, I've never seen a ghost before," she says, soft. "It's not like I had a lot of context to base my reactions off of."

He nods again.

LONELY.

"I bet, " she murmurs. "I bet, that's...rough."

He nods, settling in on the couch next to her with a brush of cold air.

"Hey," she starts, "why don't you fall through the couch? And why do you use the stairs?"

He rolls his eyes.

CAN'T FLY.

Then,

I DON'T KNOW THE RULES.

"Me neither," she replies. "Me neither."

7

After shaking off the haze of the late night, Grace gets back to work on the wall, taking the measurements again for the wall of bookshelves and finally putting in the order for it.

She'll definitely need help installing it, but that's hardly anything new for big pieces of furniture and such. And then it'd be even better to get her equipment again.

On an afterthought, she adds another grounded lamp to her list. She sees glimpses of Rodrick, but not steady, but she pays no attention.

She has no idea if he's...conscious when she can't see him. If he still exists, or if he only exists in the bursts when he's visible.

Though he said he is lonely, so he must have...some concept of time. Or something.

Springing up out of the overstuffed chair, she takes a few more measurements, writing them down.

"I'm going to go to the store, I'll be back," she says, and he seems to flicker into existence next to her computer.

She cranes her neck to type his words.

SAFE?

"Should be, I don't even have to leave town for this, just running to the hardware store."

He nods, as if he doesn't buy her words, but just watches as she backs the truck out again.

～

HOME DEPOT IS, as always, full of way more men than women, and they all think that they know more than her. Which they do not.

Especially since all she's doing is making a workbench, which is like...the first project you make when setting up a shop, and she's set up so many by this point the idea that some helper could know more is laughable.

But she spends her time picking out the wood for the top, indulging herself in how grand she can make it, how she doesn't have to worry about it fitting in a limited space, how she can make it just as short as she wants to cause it's her fucking shop, not the shop of 6 foot tall men.

As if summoned by her being in a hardware store, her phone dings.

TRIXIE (3:44 PM): Are you back on site on Tuesday?

GRACE (3:46 PM) Planning so.

TRIXIE (3:46 PM) Cause that car was waiting for you but left when your truck didn't come.

Her blood runs cold for a moment, before she forces herself to breathe and stare at some really fine oak that would probably be less than practical but really fucking lovely for a bench.

GRACE (3:52 PM): I'll figure it out.

TRIXIE (3:52 PM): If they follow me I'm calling the police.

GRACE (3:53 PM): Good idea.

She tucks the phone in her purse and stares hard at the woods, before getting a giant slab of maple and getting some help putting it in her cart, along with proper braces and some pine for legs.

Afterwards, with her truck full of lumber and finishing wax and braces and everything that makes her happy, she stops by the old storage unit and gets her circular saw, her band saw, and a few other excellent pieces, loading them up in her truck.

And despite all the heaviness and the terror of Rey and his goons, there's a lightness in her stomach, something going right, something she has control over.

So when she pulls into her warehouse and rolls up the interior door to see Rodrick standing in the middle of the rough concrete floor, pointing directly to a place on the wall, the crash is even more astronomical.

She kicks open her truck door, closing the outside door and rolling down the interior probably faster than is safe, her hands shaking as she re-padlocks the gate.

"What do you mean, they were here?" The words tumble out of her mouth, faster than what makes sense. She rechecks the lock again, making sure it's secure, then goes to where her shotgun still rests in the bucket by the door, checking it. Still loaded.

He points again, at the spot, then drifts to the laptop, cause of course he can't talk to her yet and she has to moderate her expectations because of course this can't be easy.

"Did they get in?" She blurts out, and he shakes his head, then points at the laptop.

She picks it up, her hands shaking, and he sits next to her, so close she can feel the cold roiling off of him like a bitter wind.

DID NOT GET IN.

She heaves a big sigh, and scrubs her hands over her eyes. He patiently waits for her to have a moment, then resumes their weird typing thing.

LOOKED IN WINDOWS. RATTLED DOOR. CURSED A LOT.

She tips her head back against the couch, squeezing her eyes shut. They didn't get in, they couldn't know for sure she is there, it's not a for sure thing...

But why would they look if they didn't think she's here?

"Fuck," she says out loud, then, again, because it feels good. "Fuck."

She feels a phantom finger in her side, like a cold wind is poking her, and she opens her eyes again to see Rodrick pointing at the laptop again.

THEY CALLED YOUR NAME.

"How long ago were they here?" She asks, her blood going cold once more. Then, "How'd I feel you poking me?"

He rolls his eyes at the question, then types, almost laying his hands on top of hers to poke at the buttons.

TIME DOESN'T MAKE SENSE.

She wrinkles her nose at that sentence, but he continues.

AFTER YOU LEFT BUT BEFORE YOU CAME BACK. TIME IN BETWEEN BOTH WAS THE SAME?

He even points to the question mark, and she thinks she gets it.

"So right in the middle of when I was gone?"

He nods, fervently.

She might've even passed them coming down the mountain when she came up. They might've seen the truck, turned around, and —

Again, the phantom pressure of cold, and she opens her eyes again to see him resting a hand lightly on her bare arm, his eyes eager. He mouths something to her, but it's only the barest suggestion of whispers on the wind.

"I'm okay, I'm okay, I'm just...freaking out slightly." She straightens, looks around her warehouse. "I'm gonna...make sure that the windows are locked."

He trails behind her as she drags her step ladder up to check the ancient hinges.

On most of the tall, 1930 style windows, the hinges have been rusted shut, and their bolts are still in place, as if merged with them.

The ones she's been able to open before, they're still firmly closed, their modern locks holding well.

"I'm surprised they didn't throw a brick through the window."

Rodrick bares his teeth at those words, and she gets the sudden feeling that he would...not react well if that happened.

She looks up at the light streaming through them, then sighs, heavily, cause what the fuck is she able to do. What the fuck is she ever able to do. She can't use the testimony of a ghost to the police, she can't press charges for someone rattling her windows, and Rey was still in prison.

"He's still in prison, he can't get to me."

Rodrick gestures, expansive, at the entire warehouse, and she doesn't know if that's a warning or if he's being reassuring.

Slowly, she drifts back to the couch, her heart thudding, too much, and she squeezes her eyes shut before pulling out her phone.

GRACE (5:23 PM) He sent thugs to my house. They didn't get in.

DEBORAH (5:23 PM): Still have that shotgun?

GRACE (5:24 PM): Yes.

DEBORAH (5:24 PM): The flying monkeys cometh.

Rodrick reads over her shoulder, his eyebrows crawling up, and before he even has to point she picks up her laptop.

FLYING MONKEYS?

"Did you ever see the movie Wizard of Oz?"

He gives her a quizzical look.

"Oh my god have you ever seen a movie?"

He shakes his head, slow, and Grace stares at him for a few seconds.

"Well my TV is getting here in a few days, I'm totally gonna set up Netflix and you can just watch all day," she says, then, "Do you know what movies are?"

He rolls his eyes again.

I WAS POOR. NOT STUPID.

"Great," she says, her mind casting around for anything to focus on that's not about the possible threat to her home and being. "Well the internet is gonna break your mind. We are gonna have such movie marathons."

She sees his shoulders shake, and she realizes he's laughing. At her, at the world, at the situation, she doesn't know. But laughing.

Cracking what is probably a weak and feeble smile back, she looks at her truck, still very laden with wood and equipment.

DEBORAH (5:38 PM): I'm coming over. I'm sleeping on that couch again. You don't have a choice.

Grace tilts the phone to let Rodrick know, and he nods in receipt.

GRACE (5:39 PM): Only if you help me unload my truck.

WHEN DEBORAH ARRIVES, she stares at the truck with something approaching trepidation.

"Good god, why?" She says, but she tosses her hair up into a bun and accepts the gloves Grace hands her.

It's soothing, the use of muscles and the easily seen effect they have on the truck load, especially after the heart pounding and adrenaline of earlier. Rodrick flicks along the outside of her vision, his face neutral, as if he's observing and not really participating. He gives Deborah an openly curious look, though he's seen her twice before, as if he is only really noticing her now.

She can almost see the list of questions he's forming in his brain.

After the truck, with much swearing and stumbling and dropping pieces of wood, is unloaded, Deborah meticulously does the same circle Grace did with the windows. "I'm glad they couldn't get through the door, though," she says, her voice full of frustration. "Though with a brick and a ladder they could just be...bam...inside."

"Yeah, I know," Grace says, rummaging through her fridge for dinner makings. It's not like she planned for dinner for two, and last minute panic meals are never glamorous, but she still feels the compulsive need to feed her skinny little sister. "It's gonna be rice and red beans, that okay?"

"Duh," Deborah says, not looking at her, but instead standing near the overstuffed chair. "Did you ever find that draft?"

Grace steals a glance over to where Rodrick is idling by the door, his eyes unfocused. "Nope, but it's kinda nice when it's warm."

"I just...don't want them to come in that way." Deborah says, lines creasing in her face. "Cause what if it's a crack or a weakness or..."

"I doubt the thugs are gonna squeeze through the cracks in the wall. How's work?"

Deborah narrows her eyes back at her. "Don't think you can get out of talking about this." She warns, her voice rough. "I know you. You're trying to imagine it didn't happen."

That's not fair. "I'm trying to not have panic attacks, that's different." She defends. "Rehashing all this isn't going to help it stop."

"What'll stop it is if he gets shanked in prison," Deborah mutters, her voice nasty. Deborah gets nasty when it comes to her sister's danger, and it's this harsh sort of nasty. The sort of nasty where you wouldn't be terribly surprised if someone's tires get slashed, or if they end up in a ditch.

It's heartwarming.

Sometimes.

"Yes, well, he's white, it's less likely to happen," Grace says, and the bitterness slips unwelcome into her voice, coloring it. "And you'd think it would've happened by now."

Deborah's face twists, and even thoughts she's the younger sister, she is always the sister to pull no punches when defending family. There was more than one occasion in elementary school when Grace's bullies got roughed up by her three years younger sister.

Rodrick's eyebrows, in the corner, are raised delicately, and she can't blame him. He at least appears white, and is probably pretty unaware of the racial makeup and situation in the country.

With a rush, she realizes he probably doesn't even know about WW2, which is just fucking weird.

"Can you get cameras?" Deborah asks, sudden. "I'll pay for web cameras set up here. So you can check when not home."

She blinks at her. "I mean, I don't see why not, I got good internet," Grace says, automatic. "The electricity itself isn't always the best, but internet is decent."

In the corner, Rodrick rolls his eyes again.

Deborah nods, finally satisfied with her inspection, and joins her to lean against the stove as she mixes the pot. "It'll be an early Christmas present," she says, and her voice is final. "That's in like two months, it'll be fine." She scowls. "You're accepting it. I'll let you install it, cause you do that shit, but you're accepting it."

Grace nods, cause really, what the hell is she actually going to do otherwise.

Deborah watches her stir the pot, still scowling, and Grace gets a pang of guilt. Everything with Rey hurt everyone, but in her family she often feels that her sister took the brunt of it. Took the brunt of the guilt, of the stress, of the worry, and of the constant sense that now you need to look out for someone who you thought was an adult, where you can't trust their judgements, cause their judgement got them into such a colossally bad situation before.

Grace sure as hell has trouble trusting her own judgement, and can't really blame her sister for sharing that feeling.

"I wonder," her sister starts, then stops, face falling back into the frown. "I wonder if they think you'll testify again."

"He'd have to be charged again," Grace says, her blood running cold. Of course, the thing they got Rey for had nothing to do with her, but she can't help but think her portrayal of him and how he treated her helped reduce his sentence at all.

Her sister shrugs, but her shoulders are pinched tight...she's just as upset about this as anyone would be. "Have you gone back to the therapist?"

Grace coughs, not missing the pointed look from Rodrick in the corner. "Not in the last few weeks," she says, simple. Of course, she could always pick up her phone and schedule an emergency meeting, but the stubborn part in her doesn't like the idea of going backwards.

Of course, entirely buying this place could be argued as a step backwards in some people's eyes, but she resolutely doesn't think of that. Cause that's a little bit bullshit, to frame every decision as something done in response.

But isn't that what her life is, at this point? Even when she doesn't mean to, every decision of hers is framed around whether or not it'll keep her safe.

Her sister settles into a frown as Grace serves up some pretty standard rice and beans. "Have you been...eating correctly?" Deborah asks, faltering.

Out of the corner of her eye, she sees Rodrick drift closer to them, deliberate, as if he's hoping her sister will just blurt out things again and he'll learn more.

"Yeah, yeah, even spent the night over at a friend's house the other day."

"You have friends again?" Deborah brightens, and Grace would be mad if it isn't a fair statement. "That's great! Who are they?"

"Just people from work, I've worked on a bunch of projects with them and they're, you know, nice." It feels like an incomplete statement, and her pride still burns a little at the jab.

Deborah nods, though, enthused for her sad sack of a sister. "That's fantastic! Keep at it!" Her enthusiasm is more than a little insulting, but she can't blame her.

After she left Rey -- escaped Rey -- all of her friends from before had moved on, had checked out, or were plain uninterested in accepting any apologies or overtures from her, and she had been mostly alone. People either didn't believe her, didn't think she was blameless, or didn't, you know, have the emotional energy to fully deal with all of her fallout from the crash of being in a controlling relationship. Deborah was her only family member who believed her, and the only one who continuously showed any sort of support, as skeptical and as biting as it is.

So...yeah. Saying she has friends now is a step up and probably a relief to Deborah.

Deborah snaps her fingers in front of her face, and Grace flinches back.

"You dazed off there, everything cool?"

Grace nods, fakes a smile, because of course she does because of course she can. "Yeah, just thinking."

AFTER SHE THROWS a blanket over her little sister conked out on the couch, Rodrick follows her up the stairs, a profoundly blank look on his face.

She gives him a questioning look, and he shrugs, before poking around the loft as she gets ready for bed.

But, as she tucks herself into the plush comforter, he sits on the floor next to her bed, leaning against it.

"Are you okay?" She whispers, leaning a hand down near him.

He reaches out, and there's the phantom pressure of his grasp, realer than before, much more real than she would think possible. Slowly, he nods.

It's the nod that no, he's not entirely okay, but also nothing is entirely wrong. It's the nod of someone who has no clue what to say, and it shows.

"I guess I'm a mess sometimes, right?" She whispers, rolling onto her stomach so she can look at him better in the dim light.

He nods again, but it's somehow not mean.

"Sorry the person who bought your place turned out to be so odd."

He tilts his head at her, so she can see his face, then obviously rolls his eyes.

"Right. Right." She says, and he cracks a smile at her. "Goodnight?"

He nods back, mouthing the word goodnight back at her.

SHE AWAKES AGAIN to a far away whisper, but as she lays awake and strains her ears, she can't hear anything more.

THE NEXT MORNING, her sister solemnly hands her a few more boxes of shotgun shells before she leaves, and Grace tucks one into the umbrella holder where her gun sits and one underneath her truck seat.

Not that she actively wants to shoot someone, but sometimes the mere presence of a gun will stop them. Not always, but sometimes. Enough of the time.

Rodrick watches her as she loads up work equipment in her truck with narrowed eyes.

"I'll be safe. Probably," she jokes, which does not help his scowl. "I doubt they'd do anything overt to me, I'll park the truck a bit of a distance away and then Uber to my job site." She flashes her phone at him. "Trixie said she'll tell me if they're there in the morning, that way I'll be able to avoid parking."

His lips twist, an unhappy tilt down the side.

"I know, it's shitty."

He nods fervently.

"But I mean, there's not much else I can do. I can't...not go to work."

He seems to see-saw, seriously evaluating if she did.

"I mean, I still need to eat. And pay for electricity." She smiles at him, he wrinkles his nose back.

THANK GOD, nothing happens that day. The tiny sedan isn't there, and no one follows her or Trixie home.

AND IT CONTINUES for the entire week: no trace of anyone following her, anyone trying to find her, no one seems to contact her friends or her family and it's...creepy.

8

One night, she wakes up with a jolt, her heart thudding in her chest like it wants to escape, sheets tangled.

"What?" She blurts.

It's pitch black out, and she fumbles with her little reading lamp, pulse pounding in her ears.

"Rodrick?" She clutches her lamp to her, flipping it on.

Warm light fills her loft, but she doesn't see Rodrick, then --

"Wake up!" It's a rough, far away voice, male, as if shouted into the wind.

"I'm awake! I'm awake! What?" She scrambles to her feet, holding the lamp above her head, and then —

Someone pounds on her door, the interior door rattling and shaking.

In front of it stands Rodrick, his feet rooted in the ground, eyes wide and panicked. He shoots her a look, full of anger and frustration, then eyeballs the door.

The door rattles again, and she scrambles down the spiral staircase, still in just her tank top and pajama shorts, and immediately grabs her shotgun from the umbrella stand.

Rodrick gives her a wide eyed look.

"Have they been here long?" She asks, the words falling from her mouth, as if she has much more control than she actually does.

Hands shaking, she rackets the shotgun.

He shakes his head, and the entire door quakes, as if they have a battering ram and are trying to break the lock by sheer force of power.

"Oh my god," she whispers, backing away from the door, until her back hits her truck.

Rodrick stares at the door, at the shaking, and then one by one the lights flicker on, spilling illumination over the entire warehouse. They swing, flickering, terrifying.

The rattling stops, and for a split second her heart is in her throat, as if they went away and her problem is solved, then —

"Grace?" A gruff voice echoes through the door, and her blood runs cold.

It's Mikey, Rey's second in command. And by second in command, she means he's the one who did the things that Rey didn't legally want on his hands, and yet still somehow skirts along the outside of the law.

He never laid a harmful hand on Grace, but that does not mean he didn't drag her places. Never bruised her, but always made her go where she did not want to go.

She closes her eyes at the memories hitting her like a slap.

"Open the door, Grace," he calls out, and to hear him this clearly they must have broken open the exterior door. Another thing she'll have to replace, and quickly.

Her phone's over on the giant industrial stove, so she shakily goes to it.

"I'll call the police if you don't leave," she calls back out. "I am armed, and this is private property. You are not authorized to be here," she falters, not knowing what to say or do next.

There's stillness from outside, and she takes a deep breath. One, two.

"We need to speak to you," he calls back through the door, his voice somehow more muted. "It's urgent."

"I have no wish to speak to you, and I can get a court order to prevent you from coming within 100 yards of me," she says, her heart pounding.

Rodrick is shaking, practically vibrating, his eyes wide, shaking his head.

"You need to leave," she says, loud.

And, miraculously, the door stops shaking.

Footsteps, moving away, then a slam of a car door, and squealing tires.

She stares at the door, the shotgun nestled into her shoulder still, for far too long, before the lights slowly flicker off.

Legs aching from holding them still too long, she goes to the light switch to actually, you know, turn them on instead of however they drew energy through Rodrick's fuckery.

Rodrick doesn't stop staring at the door, his eyes wide and face gaunt. He's unmoving, more akin to a statue than the animated...ghost...she had gotten used to.

She slowly, ever so slowly, puts the shotgun back into the umbrella holder.

"Rodrick?" She asks, the words feeling dry in her mouth. "Are you..."

All at once he snaps out of his frozen state, and rushes to her, the cold from him hitting her like a brick.

"I'm okay, I'm okay," she says, as he rests his hands somehow on her shoulders, the vague pressure reassuring. "I think he left."

He mouths at her, and she's not sure if she's getting better at reading lips or if she can actually hear him say "who?"

"It's Rey's best friend, my...ex's best friend. I don't know why he'd...why he'd come."

Rodrick's eyes search her face, as if trying to find something in her words, before he steps away, the pervasive cold dripping away.

Grace takes a deep breath, then another, then another, then all but stumbles to the couch. "Jesus fuck what time is it?"

She flips her phone over, and it's just before five AM.

"Fuck." She leans her head on the back of the couch, her heart pounding, and she practices her calming breathing. Which always feels like bullshit, but whatever. Has to be done.

Rodrick stands near her, and when she opens her eyes again, he tentatively points to the laptop.

"Yeah, yeah, good idea." She drags it over to herself, that strange, jittery feeling of adrenaline coating every motion. She's so jittery she can feel it in her teeth.

Opening the word doc with all their current conversations, he watches her for a split second, before poking at the keys.

LONG SENTENCE

She nods. "So don't interrupt?"

He barely nods in response, before poking at the keys, and she starts to type, not letting her mind string together the words until he's done.

It's a strange peace of just pressing keys, especially so soon after the shaking and the rattling and pressing the gun so hard into her shoulder, that she almost zones out until she realizes he's stopped poking at the keys and is giving her just the most concerned look.

She shakes herself, and actually looks at the screen.

HE KNOCKED FIRST. THEN SHOOK LOCK, THEN BROKE IT. JUST ONE PERSON OUT THERE. HE YELLED FOR YOU, MANY TIMES. YOU DIDN'T WAKE UP. HE STARTED SHAKING THE DOOR, THEN HIT IT WITH SOMETHING. THE BUILDING SHOOK. YOU CAME DOWN, AND HE STARTED USING A BRICK AGAINST THE EXTERIOR LOCK.

He's looking at her expectantly to finish, then goes back to poking at the keys.

HE WAS YELLING THAT HE HAD MONEY FOR YOU.

"At 5 AM? Then he can call my lawyer. During the day," she says, mouth numb. "What the fuck."

He shrugs, eyes still wide.

"Are you okay? You got all...still."

I DIDN'T WANT HIM IN.

"No kidding, me neither."

He narrows his eyes at her, as if her response is slightly frustrating, but she really doesn't care if he thinks she's frustrating right now.

Pulling the throw blanket over her on the couch, she curls up, condemning herself to a lost night of no more sleep. "I don't know what's happening right now," she says, feeling small.

He pokes at the keyboard, and she types, face already feeling like it's throbbing.

TECHNOLOGY HAS CHANGED SINCE ME.

She snorts a bit, and he smiles at her, sly.

CAN TECHNOLOGY DO SOMETHING TO HELP?

She stares at his words, until they blur together, an indistinct mess of ideas and half possibilities.

WHEN MORNING HAS COME and bright white light streams through the high windows and it's no longer rude to text people, she picks up her phone with a deep breath.

GRACE (9:08 AM): So you also do a lot of wiring, right?

There's no immediate response, so she drags herself up to the loft and changes into her work jeans and a flannel shirt. Cause the least she can do in all of this is putter around.

She's noticing, definitely, that Rodrick is never looking at her when she changes. Out of some misguided sense of chivalry or politeness she doesn't know.

Downstairs, her phone beeps, so she shoves her feet into work boots and clatters down the stairs.

TRIXIE (9:17 AM): Yes!!! But no one asks me because I do lighting!! But yes!! I love it!!

GRACE (9:18 AM): You working today? Want a consult on a strange space?

Rodrick flickers over her shoulder, reading the texts, before shooting her a disappointed look.

"She's the one that warned me when I was followed to work,"

Grace murmurs, pocketing her phone and picking up her pliers. "She let me crash on her couch."

His mouth twists, but he shrugs instead of doing anything else.

TRIXIE (9:20 AM): Um sure? Address? Anything I should bring?

GRACE (9:21 AM) Bring any wiring kit that can help with home security?

TRIXIE (9:23 AM): I have demos.

Grace again pockets her phone and, hand shaking and shotgun easily available, she unlocks the interior door and rolls it open.

The crisp autumn morning air hits her, despite the flannel and the boots, and she shivers a bit.

The exterior door lock is sheared off, the padlock broken and the bolt laying on the ground outside, on the rough blacktop.

Outside, in her strange little neighborhood of abandoned warehouses, Condos, and office buildings nestled in the town at the foot of the hills of Southern California, no one moves. It's like, for this one morning moment, that she's the only person in existence.

Even though Rodrick is watching her with sharp eyes from the door.

"I'll have to replace it, and fortify the door." She says, inspecting the broken edge of the door. "I mean, I can do that in my sleep, it's just pricy. To do it properly."

He's obviously looking around outside, his eyes narrow as if he is suddenly nearsighted.

Sighing, she picks up a chunk of broken concrete and props the door open, before coming back inside and rolling down the interior door.

Cause even though it's day, doesn't mean they might not come back. So she padlocks it again as well.

It takes a good hour to get to her place from Los Angeles, so she tidies up, strangely nervous about a work associate actually stepping foot in her home. Her work bench is only half done, with the leg brackets setting, and she takes a shop vac to the area in a vain hope to get rid of some of the pervasive sawdust, working up a bit of a sweat despite the chill of the air.

So when the door rattles with her knocking, she jumps, before eyeing Rodrick.

He nods at her, his face relaxed and unworried.

"Can you tell who it is?" She whispers as she crosses to the door.

Again, he nods.

So she plasters on a grin and rolls up the interior door, revealing Trixie with hilariously wide eyes.

"Jesus Christ, what is this place?" She breathes, stepping in. Her sharp eyes fly to the loft, to the industrial stove, to the half finished wall and the workbench, before she twists to face Grace. "This is it. This is your space."

"Yeah," she says, a small smile threatening to break out. "Bought it on the cheap."

Trixie presses a hand against the brick of the wall, near one of the vaulted windows. "This is amazing," she breathes out, knocking her knuckles against the wall. "How the fuck did you find this?"

Grace gestures her further in, and she springs inside, all but spinning to look around.

"Those beams, mid 20s? Late 20s?"

"1928! Earthquake fitted in early 70s, though."

From where he stands near the overstuffed chair, Rodrick beams at her. As if he is somehow proud of her for that.

Trixie goes over to the shop space, where the in-progress bench lays. "This is so ace I can't even believe it," she says, a joyous tilt to her voice. "I've seen some of those designs out of New York, I never even thought this could be in California."

"I had to search a bit, but they exist." Grace grins at Trixie, who returns it.

"And you're gonna make this into a shop? With the whole space thing and...a half wall?"

"It's going to be a book cube wall, I'm getting a discount, just fixing the base of it so it's not as wobbly."

Trixie pauses from her marveling to give her a look, and it's the look of someone who wants an answer. "And you need help wiring up a security system why?"

There it is. "Because those guys waiting behind our cars at the Beverly Hills job tried to get in last night at 5 AM," she answers, wincing at the honesty. "And I want to be able to see who it is by camera -- remotely if possibly -- instead of guessing."

Trixie blinks once, twice, then visibly moves on. "Do you have exterior electrical hookups or just interior?"

"Just interior right now."

She looks to where Grace's truck is parked, as if making a few mental calculations and finding the answer incomplete. "I mean a nest doorbell could be a start, but..."

"But easily broken. I was thinking window as well."

Trixie nods, absent minded, her eyes sharp and inspecting the windowsill, standing on her tiptoes to do so. "Unless you have a problem with glare I can set some up on each window, probably," she says, voice distracted. "How's the electricity? Stable?"

Grace and Rodrick share a glance, and he grins at her, as if it's the funniest thing ever. "Generally." You know, unless Rodrick got upset. Which he probably would if someone tried to get in again, it seems to have that effect.

Trixie hmmms, then cranes her neck up to the high vaulted ceiling. "Think you could set up solar? It might be easier to custom wire than the city grid. And more difficult to hijack...does it snow up here?"

"We are not nearly high up enough the mountain for it to snow, that's like Big Bear levels, not this."

She nods absentmindedly, then finally sets her duffel onto the overlong table Grace bought. She takes a moment to run her hands over the table, before digging into the bag. "I still can't believe you get to make this place so custom," she says, marveling. "Please tell me you're not covering the brick."

"Oh hell no, I love the brick."

"Good! Not enough people here do!"

"It's the earthquakes."

Trixie unravels a bunch of cords and electronic equipment from her bag, and Rodrick drifts closer, peering in curiosity. Not animosity, thank god, but it is his idea so it'd be a bit silly if he got territorial with this.

"The easiest quick fix is the nest doorbell, we can hook that into your cell, so if anyone knocks on the door or rings it you'll get a notification. And, you know, vocally answer it from anywhere," Trixie says, placing it to one side.

For a split second her face creases, as if she's distressed and about to cry, before it smoothes over back into the professional expression she wears all the goddamn time.

"Next I have a few cameras we can point out, and they should record well as long as the lights aren't blaring on in here." Trixie holds up two tiny, CCTV style cameras. "I can't really hook these up to your phone without modifications, but those can come later."

Rodrick's halfway through the table to look at them, and it's a surreal thing she's still not used to; seeing someone's body half bisected by an object yet still reacting to things.

"But really, can I see the roof?" Trixie puts down the equipment. "I assume you had it inspected?"

"Oh, fully, but I don't have a ladder that goes up to it that easily," she says, then gestures with her thumb. "You can reach the ceiling beams from the loft, if ya wanna see."

"Fuck yeah," Trixie says, enthused beyond belief. "I love these old pieces of shit."

Rodrick gives her such an offended look she has issues not laughing, but he still follows them up the spiral staircase.

Trixie whistles when she sees how much they can see from the loft. "Jesus Christ," she whispers, leaning over the wiring railing. "What was this?"

"Overseer's office, near as I can tell," Grace says, shooting a look to Rodrick for confirmation. He nods.

"Makes something resembling sense." She tests her feet on the hardwood. "Original?"

"Realtor said mid-60s reno." At Rodrick's nod, she continues. "But it's nice and smooth so I don't care."

"Most 60s flooring did tile?" Trixie says, squatting to inspect it.

"This one liked old stuff, I think," Grace says with a shrug, sitting on her bed.

After a few seconds, Trixie finds what she's looking for and cranes her neck to the ceiling and the large metal beams that race across the ceiling. Grace lets her lose herself in the inspection, and instead watches Rodrick.

Rodrick peers at Trixie with something akin to curiosity and something akin to concern, as if he's entirely uncertain about her being up here. As if he doesn't necessarily mind, but it's entirely cool with the idea of someone new up in her loft.

A small thought pillows its way into her heart. She's gonna have to ask him if he minds the intrusion, or if he welcomes the distraction from the long loneliness he's had so far.

He doesn't seem to mind her, now. Especially now that they've found the laptop to communicate with.

Almost on cue, Grace's cell phone beeps, and Trixie pays her absolutely zero attention as she pulls it out.

HEATHER PSYCHIC GIRL (2:15 PM): Anything new?

With a jolt, Grace realizes she never told her about the laptop or...or really anything.

GRACE (2:15 PM): Oh yes. Talk later?

HEATHER PSYCHIC GIRL (2:16 PM): !!!! Yes!!!

Rodrick gives her a dirty look, which will be another thing to talk about when Trixie isn't here.

She's getting tired of having to have all these secret conversations so she doesn't look insane, but whatever.

"I'm surprised by the lack of rust on these," Trixie chimes in, still distracted. "A lot of these old buildings have issues with that in the beams."

Rodrick shrugs at Grace.

"I dunno, but the realtor said that it had been well cared for."

After a split second Rodrick seems to shrug into himself, shrink down, as if ashamed, and she leans into him. Sorta. Would've knocked shoulders with him if he was a physical being, but as it is she just leans until that brief moment of phantom pressure doesn't give way.

He all but leans back, his head on her shoulder, and he almost feels like a real person.

Trixie eventually shrugs, before jumping lightly. "This loft is solid," she says, her voice a bit amazed in the way that gives Grace a warm feeling inside. "I love this."

"And it's mine," Grace says, a smile breaking out on her face. "It's mine and I still can't believe I got it."

"What sort of wall you doing over there?"

Grace heads down the stairs, and they follow her, with Rodrick still giving the unreadable glances to Trixie as they walk.

Her phone beeps again.

HEATHER PSYCHIC GIRL (2:55 PM): Can I come over tonight?

GRACE (2:55 PM): Sure.

Grace flips open her laptop and easily navigates to her planning document, where she has the wall saved. Trixie cranes her neck to look, nodding in recognition.

"Did you get that from that one store in Bev Hills?" She asks, pointing at the screen.

"Got the idea, yes, sure as hell didn't buy it there."

Trixie looks over to the drywall wall with a nod. "So you just made the base?"

"Pretty much, wanted a more stable set up for earthquakes, you know?" Grace can just feel herself smiling so hard, it's like the last night didn't even happen.

Except, of course, now that she's had the thought, the feeling of being watched and people outside crawls back up her spine. "Can we set up the cameras now? Or is it a later sort of thing?"

Trixie blinks, owlish, at her. "I mean sure?" It's like she forgot the original reason for coming, for being summoned an hour out of LA on a Thursday. "I mean, it's like the easiest thing ever."

So they spend the next few hours hooking up, troubleshooting with her phone, and setting up the exterior cameras.

After swinging the exterior door open and shut a few times and seeing the utterly useless lock, Trixie gives her a raised eyebrow look. "Think you need to get a new door," she says dryly, fiddling with the broken lock mechanism. "Something that's not gonna fragment like this."

"I'm thinking fiberglass security doors," she says, flexing the wood doors and showing how flimsy they are. They bow in her hands. "I mean, a really determined six year old could get through these."

"Mmm, nine," Trixie says, a furrow over her brow but a smile on her face. "That's when they get all coordinated."

"Thank god for the roll up door," Grace blurts out. "That thing's not going anywhere."

Trixie's eyebrows raise, but she nods, before turning another screw attaching the nest doorbell. "And this should work, and if it doesn't we need to contact corporate cause this was an advertising freebie." She smiles, but it's a disturbed smile, a fake smile. "I already had one, so I just saved it."

"You had one of these on an apartment?"

"I loved them in the big houses so I thought..." She shrugs. "Why not, right?"

"Sure."

THAT NIGHT, the doorbell rings and Grace is able to pull up the tiny fish-eye camera on her phone to reveal Heather standing there, shifting foot to foot. "See?" She shows Rodrick. "This'll help."

He squints at it, but doesn't try to stop her from going to the door to roll it up.

Heather eyes the entire room, as if it is a slightly toxic environment. "Wow you changed like everything," she says, something judgy in her voice. "And your ghost is okay with it?"

She glances at Rodrick, who shrugs, nonplussed. "Yeah he's cool."

Heather seems vaguely impressed, before eyeing her sharply, but her eyes slide off her quickly. Like the vague idea of eye contact is unpalatable. "Well, the entire place seems less hostile," she says, her voice small. "So whatever you're doing different is probably working.

"We figured out how to talk with the laptop," Grace says, almost wanting to reassure her. "It works for conversations."

Heather tilts her head, staring roughly where Rodrick is standing. "He's okay with that?"

Rodrick nods enthusiastically.

"He's nodding right now, so I think that's good. Here..." She picks up the laptop and, with a glance to Rodrick, opens up a brand new Word document. "He points to the keys and I type, and then I get to see his full sentences."

Her eyebrows flash up. "Really?" She breathes, eyes wide. "So you can ask him questions and shit?"

"And he can tell me when things happen here when I'm gone, and...random shit."

Rodrick rolls his eyes, then starts poking at the keyboard, but she's nowhere near it.

"Wait, he's saying something, just a sec." She sits down, settling in, and Rodrick starts over typing again.

TELL HER TO NOT BRING IN THE HAND SCANNER.

Grace tilts the screen to Heather, who scowls, looking briefly guilty. "It's in my bag, it doesn't hurt him."

He pokes at the keyboard again, with more strength than necessary.

IT'S ANNOYING AND SOUNDS LOUD.

Heather's lips thin, before she pushes herself up. "Would it help if I put it in my car?"

Rodrick nods, so Grace nods, and Heather tromps to the door in her combat boots. After a muffled noise of a car door slamming, Heather comes back in, sans messenger bag.

"How'd you know I had it in my bag?"

LOUD.

Heather's eyes steal over to Grace for a split second, the split second that Grace is quickly becoming accustomed to. "Do you know what a hand scanner is?" She asks, accusatory.

"Not a clue."

"It picks up on extra sensory rays and then vibrates in the palm of my hand. I have never had a ghost be able to tell me it's annoying." If anything, she just looks grumpy for not knowing about it. "God, that's fucking the worst."

Rodrick's shoulders are less tight looking and further away from his ears.

Without her bag, she looks small, slouched in on herself. "So. All this is an improvement, I think?" Heather says, her voice muted. As if the items in the bag were keeping her sane and confident. "Are you getting along? Any more lightbulb explosions?"

"No, it's been fine." She looks over at Rodrick, who shrugs and nods.

"Does he still mess with the electricity?"

Again the eye roll, like she's used to, and he starts poking at the keyboard.

I CAN'T CONTROL THAT.

Heather cranes her neck at the screen, and with Rodrick sitting next to her, it's almost too much close people. "Can I...can I just ask a bunch of questions?"

Rodrick rolls his eyes, holds up three fingers.

"He says three."

Heather sits back, face profoundly blank, as if she never thought this day would come, and, now that it has, has no clue what the fuck to say. "Um," she says, eyes wide and racing. "Uhhh."

Rodrick flashes a smile to Grace, and starts poking at the keys.

UNLESS THAT IS TOO MANY.

Heather squints. "Is he being funny? Is he funny? Is the one ghost who's developed enough to hold a conversation that I could ask someone who is funny?"

"Pretty much," Grace says while Rodrick nods.

"I've never actually gotten a chance to ask a question! They're always too...combative. Or angry. Or or or..." She looks down, over-whelmed. "Are you sure I can ask questions?"

Rodrick nods, so Grace nods, feeling like an odd conduit between two people's strange breakdown in communication.

"Do you feel pain now?" Heather blurts.

Rodrick sits back, visibly taken aback by the question. He locks eyes, wide, with Grace, as if she is at fault for such a question. He takes a long moment, before he starts to hit keys, slowly, falteringly.

I DON'T THINK SO? SOMETIMES I THINK I DO, BUT WHEN I REFLECT ON IT, IT WAS SOMETHING ELSE.

Heather mouths the words along with her typing, which is among the most disorienting things ever.

"Woah," she says, soft, at such a statement. "That's..." Heather leans forward to where her nose is almost touching the screen. "How the hell?"

Rodrick's face twists, and he sighs, so hard that Grace can almost hear it.

Or maybe she can hear it. The possibility that she might be able to converse with him is ever present in her mind, hanging out there, but she doesn't know where her imagination ends and reality begins.

After too long of silence, Heather clears her throat. "Are you locked in this location?"

He just nods, and Heather looks at Grace's hands expectantly.

"Oh, he just nodded, that's an easy question," she says, after the moment stretches too long. "I think I confirmed that one with him a while ago."

"Do you have any family left?"

Rodrick recoils as if struck, then furiously starts typing.

HOW AM I TO KNOW?

"Well, I'm asking cause —"

Rodrick shakes his head with a furious twist, then continues typing.

I HAD A BROTHER BUT HE LEFT TO GO TO CANADA BEFORE I DIED. MY SISTER DIED WHEN I WAS 20. I HAD NO WIFE OR KIDS, TOO POOR.

"Oh," Heather starts. "I didn't mean,"

IT WAS 80 FUCKING YEARS AGO HOW COULD I KNOW MY

BROTHER DIDN'T COME BACK TO VISIT MY FORMER WORKPLACE.

Heather covers her mouth with her hand. "You can swear?"

Rodrick sits back, crossing his arms with a final shake of his head.

On the ceiling, the lightbulb above them swings and flickers.

"Of course he can swear, swearing wasn't invented in the 1940s," Grace says, soothing, locking eyes with Rodrick in a way she hopes is soothing.

She would've never thought to ask, and is a bit glad, cause it's clearly a sore spot.

"We can try to track him down?" Heather says, tentative, her eyes tracking the swinging lightbulb. "Is that something you're interested in?"

Rodrick just sits back further, frown deepening.

"And I think he's done answering questions, Heather." Grace slowly closes the laptop, and doesn't miss the look of relief on Rodrick's face. He glances up at the lightbulb, then with a twists of his head, flickers out of existence.

It's been a bit since she's seen him disappear intentionally, but she can't really find it in herself to blame him after that.

Heather clutches at her scarf, pulling her feet underneath herself. "I offended him, didn't I? I offended him."

"Yeah he left, he does that," Grace says, the feeling that she's the only sane one in the room at the moment. "That was probably a bit of a harsh question, I think."

Heather nods, her eyes wide. "Can I apologize to him? Somehow?" Her voice pitches upwards, as if she's genuinely panicking and needs a way to feel better about this. "I'll leave something here, something ghosts like or something?"

"What do ghosts like that you can leave?" Grace asks, curious. "I mean, mostly what he likes is the grounded lamps I bought."

Heather exhales, slow. "I mean I know there are things that ghosts seem to appreciate around? I could bring those by?"

"Sure?" Grace doesn't really know how to respond, cause, well, Rodrick is always seeming a bit moody and mercurial, so she never thought to really make it up to him. Or do something that ghosts apparently like.

"Cause I don't want him to hate me, I just wanted to ask cause I thought that'd be something one could ask you know?" Heather rambles, her voice pitching up even further, as if she is panicking and needing to justify herself. "It's rough and I don't get to actually get answers from ghosts, just sort of the vague knowledge that they exist and they want something or they have moods, you know?"

Grace didn't know but isn't gonna interrupt a rant.

"And they're really actually pretty rare despite what popular culture leads you to believe and they generally only want to speak to one person -- like you -- and don't like the presence of others and it's super rare that you developed a way of communicating before you can actually talk and I thought it was so cool." She hugs herself, as if now that Rodrick is gone she's actually feeling the somewhat pervasive chill. "And no one actually knows shit about ghosts, so I wanted to know."

"Like that question about pain."

"Yeah."

"Well," Grace starts. "I know that he gets distressed sometimes," she says, trying to be gentle, cause if nothing else she has experience with emotional people who need to calm the hell down. "I know sometimes he wants comfort, is that what you mean?"

Heather eyes her. "Comfort? Like..."

"Like reassurances? That I'm here? Stuff like that?" It feels private to discuss, especially something as nebulous as the weird support thing she does for the ghost that's....mostly not even super conscious.

Heather's still panicked look does nothing to help her feel better about her skills at reassuring, though Heather takes big gulps of air like she has been without for too long. "Do you think he'd let me back?"

"Well I don't think he could stop you if he disliked you, but...I can ask later?"

"Good idea." Heather stands up so quickly it's like a bit of shock. "I'll come back later, and you can let me know when I can. Yes?"

"Uh, yes," Grace says, blinking quickly. "Yeah, sure."

And as she walks out the awkward girl, unrolling the interior door and eyeing the broken door in distaste, Heather turns back to her, sudden, the moment she steps over the door frame. "Be careful," she blurts out, then pauses, just waiting there.

The hair on the back of her arms crawling, Grace waits, then nods. "Yeah, will do."

Heather almost reaches out to touch her, but stops herself visibly. "I mean, you're in danger from something I think. I don't know what. But something?"

Grace nods again, because of course she is. She always is, as is the bitter nature of her life. "I don't really think it's the ghost doing it, really," she says, fighting hard to keep the wistfulness out of her voice. "He even helped with a little of that."

In the cold autumn air, this far up the mountain, Heather shivers as she peers at Grace, and Grace is suddenly struck by how tired and how long she's been awake. "Well, stay safe?" Heather says, tentative. "You're pretty cool, if you already have a ghost feeling that okay with you."

"Thanks."

Out of some misplaced pity or some odd responsibility, Grace watches as Heather gets into her tiny car -- of course she drives a tiny car -- and waits until she pulls out of the abandoned little industrial district, before turning inside and rolling down the interior door and triple checking the deadbolt.

Rodrick's nowhere to be found, but he does that periodically, so she gets ready for bed, bone tired and a little heart sad.

9

This time, when she wakes up in the middle of the night, it's not adrenaline pumping through her system, but the slow inorexable feeling that she shouldn't still be asleep.

She squeezes her eyes shut, and just listens.

Nothing.

Well, wait.

She strains her ears, holding her breath, and she can hear the same far away whisper, the underwater rush of a voice speaking, caught in the roar of a wind. A wind that's not shaking her building, at least.

Slowly, ever so slowly, she sits up, and in the dim light of the streetlights through the windows, she sees Rodrick sitting at the foot of her bed, an unreadable look on his face, the light partially streaming through him.

She locks eyes with him, and his mouth closes with a snap.

For a long moment, she waits to hear that voice again, but nothing.

"Was that you?" She whispers, as if the moment is momentous enough to need a whisper. It feels momentous enough, at least.

He doesn't respond at first, so she reaches a hand out to him, and he catches it, cradling it softly, as if, if he isn't careful, she will break.

Her heart pitter pattering in her chest, she watches as he moves his hand around hers, testing it, testing himself. He's solid, almost. Or at least, there's the sensation of another hand in hers, and if she closes her eyes she would believe that it's just another person.

"I can feel you," she whispers, and he jerks his head in a nod, his expression not changing from the intense concentration as he regards her hand. "I'm not sure if it's real, but I think I feel your hand."

His eyes dart to hers, but he keeps his mouth shut, as if afraid of the answer.

"I'm sorry Heather offended you, I don't think she meant it."

He half shrugs, and goes back to looking at her cradled hand in his.

"You can try to say something," Grace says, her heart in her throat, feeling as if she shouldn't say that but...that she needs to. "If it doesn't work, it doesn't work now. Doesn't mean it won't work later."

She sees his Adam apple bob as he swallows, but he says nothing. Like he's scared of the results, scared of what to say, scared of it.

She sits up closer, and he watches her, frozen. Tentative, not wanting to spook him or scare him unnecessarily, she reaches up a hand to his cheek.

He doesn't wince away, but he closes his eyes and takes a deep intake of breath. As if he breathes, instead of just aping the motion.

She doesn't know if he actually breathes or not. Or if he needs to.

The moment her hand touches his cheek, it's cold, immediately cold, like a marble statue left outside in the winter, but...but it's something. It's there, it's not some nebulous pressure.

He takes a quick intake of breath, and his eyes pop open, wide, panicked.

"Hey, it's okay," she says, cause calming skittering animals is why she lasted so long with Rey to begin with. "It's just me." That's something she used to say when he was in the middle of his panics; when the bravado and violence and fear of the man broke down to a scared little child; when, for once in their relationship, she was the one in control and he was the one who needed and craved something from her.

Rodrick narrows his eyes, as if seeing right through her statement and finding it wanting. It helps, a bit, with her. It's less like she's following in her past and more like what they actually were like in their interactions.

"You okay?" She asks, shifting her hand slightly, and he leans into her touch, like it's the only real thing he's ever felt. And it could be, after this long.

He nods, and she can feel his skin moving in her hands, real as anything she's ever felt.

Her heart pounds, sudden, at the implications. "Jesus christ I'm touching a ghost," she blurts out, and his eyes pop open in surprise. "Sorry, but..." She trails off, and he nods again, amusement crinkling around the edges of his eyes. "I mean, you're dead, and I'm touching your face."

He smiles, shy, at her, and she smiles back.

～

THE NEXT WEEK he doesn't talk, but as long as she's in the house he doesn't stop touching her either.

It's nothing rude, it's all carefully and studiously non-sexual, but he follows her around, a hand on her shoulder, a slide of fingers down her arm as if she is just fascinating, or, in quiet moments, the slow leaning of his head against her shoulder.

And all of it's done with this raw sort of wonder on his face, so open that it makes her insides hurt. Makes something hurt. Makes something feel some sort of incredible sorrow that he has been denied this for so long and some sort of joy that he is feeling it now.

It also makes going to work fucking difficult, cause each time she breaks the contact his eyes widen, as if she just struck him, harmed him, before he schools his expressions to carefully bland.

～

She's out to lunch with Trixie, in between the houses of Beverly Hills inside of a tiny diner, that fundamentally feels like it shouldn't exist, named Mari's, when Mike sits down next to them as if it's entirely okay to do.

Trixie, without missing a beat, picks up her iced tea and hurls it into his face without her expression even changing.

Grace sits there, frozen, as he sputters through the iced tea and the waitress watches, clutching the order pad to her chest.

"Please leave," Trixie says, loftily, before smiling wide at the waitress. "More iced tea?"

The waitress nods, scurrying to the back.

Mike picks up their used napkins to wipe the drink from his face, his deep set eyes narrowed, before he consciously turns to Grace, ignoring Trixie completely. "I need to talk to you."

The pit of her stomach goes cold. "No thanks," she says, and her voice only wavers a little bit.

Trixie gets the additional glass of iced tea and just...holds it, staring at Mike, as if challenging him.

But Grace knows, just knows in the pit of her stomach, that it takes a hell of a lot more than just some cold tea to dissuade him.

"It's quick, and then we will leave you alone," he says, voice tinging on desperate.

And while leaving her alone sounds just fantastic, she doesn't trust it for a moment. "I can call the police," she says, even though they both know that the moment a police officer sees him he'll be fine. "It'll be an inconvenience, if nothing else."

"Seriously, just a few minutes—"

"She's on the clock right now, you'd have to pay for her time," Trixie interrupts, her face stone cold impassive. "Her going rate is 200$ an hour, are you prepared to pay?"

Mike full on ignores her, his mouth thinning into a red line, his ginger beard pale against his skin. "He wants to see you."

Again, her blood runs cold, but if the past few years has taught her anything it's to not react when her blood is made of ice. "No."

Mike gives her a look as if she is the unreasonable one. "It's nothing big, it's nothing that you'd be upset by, he just wants to see you." His voice scrapes into the desperate, and suddenly Grace understands.

Rey had threatened him, that something would happen if she didn't come with him. It's the oldest tactic in the book, and one he would lord over her at all times.

"Who is it this time, Mikey?" She asks, slipping into the familiar as if it is nothing. "Is he threatening you sister? Your dog? Or your motorcycle?"

Mike is caught, and he knows it. "My father's company."

"Shouldn't have let him invest in it." Grace turns back to Trixie with wide eyes. "We're done here, right?"

Almost on cue, the waitress sets down their plates with their meals, as if the cosmos themselves are calling her bluff.

Still, Trixie nods, waving the waitress back. "Take out containers?" And she uses that syrupy sweet voice, the one that scares the shit out of people, the one that belays the drama queen underneath.

Mike tries to lay a hand on Grace's arm, and she shakes him off with a hard hard flinch. "It'll just be a fifteen minute conversation, it'll be safe, you can choose the location, and then you'll be done."

It's never done, it's never something she can put behind her, and she scrapes her corned beef hash into the take out container with shaking hands. "He's in jail and I will never go to that building." She stands, nodding at Trixie, whose face is a perfectly impassive mask that Grace just wishes she could emulate. "Don't follow me," she orders Mike, knowing that he'll disregard her words in a heartbeat if he is ordered to. "Tell him I want nothing to do with him, and I won't ever want anything to do with him."

Her voice quavers, of course, but with a nod to Trixie, she sweeps out of the tiny diner.

Once onto the tree studded street in Beverly Hills, with a glance to make sure he hasn't left the diner yet, Trixie yanks her into the high end appliance store on the corner. "What the fuck?" Trixie hisses out, ignoring the blond store clerk's concerned glance. "How the fuck were you that cool?"

Grace looks down at her hands, which are shaking something fierce. "Um."

Trixie pulls her deeper into the store, where they have a fake table display, and all but pushes her into the seat. "I mean, you were calm. He was threatening you, and you just...had the retorts. How the fuck?"

The blond clerk sets down a cup of water in front of Grace, as if she somehow determined that this is a dramatic moment that needed something. Grace thankfully gulps it down.

"Therapy?" Grace says, attempting a joke but it falls flat. "Practice?"

Trixie stands over her, her hands on her hips, her face a furious mask. There's a long moment, when she just stares at Grace, before sitting at the table setting next to her. "You don't really mind, do you?" She asks the blond clerk.

The blond clerk shakes her head, gesturing to the mostly empty store. "We have an appointment in forty five minutes, but as long as no one comes in, you're fine." Concern laces her voice. "Someone threatened you? In Beverly Hills?"

"It was someone I knew, it's not a big deal." Grace stares down at her shaking hands. "He's just an asshole."

"Grace, he sounded like an organized crime gooney." Trixie snaps out. "That's not how this is supposed to work."

Grace doesn't really have a reply for that, so she lets her work friend rant at her until it's time to go back to the worksite.

SHE DRIVES BACK up the mountain after picking up a new door to find Mike waiting in front of her building, leaning against his idling sedan.

He locks eyes with her, and she puts her truck into park, slowly reaching under her seat and pulling out the shotgun.

"It's cowardly to wait for someone outside their home," she calls out, holding the shotgun much more casually than she feels.

Mike's eyebrows shoot up, fast. "Where'd you pick up that?" His white undershirt is stained with the tea, and he looks even more white trash than usual.

She stares at him, her heart pounding, but the interior door is still rolled down and padlocked.

He sighs, visibly, and tries to step closer, and she lifts the shotgun to her shoulder. She doesn't know if she could actually shoot at a person, but it stops him in his tracks.

"What happened to the little lady huddling under the table whenever Rey got home?" He calls out, and she actively has to resist squeezing her eyes shut in response.

"She got out," she calls back, fitting the shotgun snugly against her shoulder.

His eyebrows raise again, slower this time, and he regards her with something resembling respect, before clearing his throat. Keeping his hands obviously where she can see them, he reaches into his car and pulls out a Manila folder.

"This is for you," he says, loud, before lowering it to the ground and placing it carefully on the crumbling asphalt. "It would be easier if you just talked to him."

"I don't do his bidding," she says, keeping it tight on her shoulder, just like her gun safety class had trained her. "If he has mail, he could always send me an email." He couldn't, cause she blocked everyone from that life's email account, but Mike didn't need to know that in the slightest.

Mike's hulking arms cross in front of his tea stained shirt. "You know he's out," he says, gruff, and her blood runs cold. "You're not going to be able to hide for forever."

Her lips thin, but she'd rather cut off her own foot than lower the gun.

He doffs his invisible cap to her, before slowly getting back into his tiny sedan and driving off.

She tracks his movement with the gun, until he turns out of the abandoned warehouse track and she can no longer hear any car noises. Then, and only then, does she release her iron grip on her shotgun and shakes out her cramped hand.

"Fuck," she whispers, before unlocking the interior door and rolling it up, then driving her truck in and closing it behind her. "Fuck."

She doesn't immediately see Rodrick and no one rang her doorbell and triggered her cell phone, so they probably didn't immediately try to get in, but she checks the recordings of all her cameras, and all they show is Mike idling outside and kicking stones while he waits.

She scrubs her hand over her face, the panic bleeding off into something way too close to exhaustion.

If Rey is out...

If Rey is already out, he would already be at her doorstep if that is something he honestly wants to do, so she has no reason to trust Mike's words.

If he is already out he would already be talking to her family, already trying to convince her sister, and already back to sweet talking her mom. There would be no reason for her to think anything else, anything otherwise, and any other course of thought is just viciously cruel to herself.

"I deserve better than to be cruel to myself," she mumbles, heart pounding. "I deserve better than to psych myself up for nothing."

As if he thought she was talking to him, Rodrick appears next to her, and immediately rests a hand on her arm.

Prickly, not wanting to be touched, she shakes him off and his eyebrows raise.

"Did you hear that? Outside?" She snaps out, and he slowly shakes his head, enough for her to get her own head out of her ass. "Wait, you didn't?" It wasn't like they were talking quietly or anything.

Again he shakes his head, wary, as if he's realizing just how upset she is.

"Can you hear anything outside?" And all the stress and fear breaks into her voice, and it wobbles.

Slow, he rests the hand back on her arm, as if being kind to a small child, and shakes his head.

She squeezes her eyes shut past the tears swelling up, outside of her control. "That guy who broke the door was back," she says, and her voice is like it is dragged over sandpaper. "He found me at lunch, and then waited out here until I got off work."

His cold hands go frantic, to her cheek, to her neck, as if checking her for injuries.

And, as if far away -- "Are you okay?"

Her eyes pop open, and she stares at him. "I heard that," she says, her mind latching onto the nearest thing that can distract it. "I heard that. You said that."

Caught in the act, he nods, but keeps his lips sealed. He raises an eyebrow, waiting for her to answer the question.

"I'm fine, he didn't touch me, but." She stares at him. "You spoke and I heard that. Do that again."

He scowls at her, then pokes at her side, his eyes unfocusing for a second, then, "Is he gone?"

She has to strain to hear his words, lean forward, but they're there. They're there and they're distinct and wonderful and she smiles at him. Sure, she's probably focusing on this to not focus on the shit going on outside, but she'll take it.

"He left, I wouldn't open my door if he was out there," she says, then reaches out and rests a hand on his shoulder.

He looks so uncomfortable with speaking that he reaches up and grasps her hand.

And Grace knows she should let him know everything but literally she doesn't want to in the slightest. "You can...actually speak now. This is great."

The look on his face shows he doesn't think of it as great but doesn't want her to stop talking about the shit going on. "Why?" It's more like a faraway whisper right now.

"Cause it'll be easier to actually understand you?"

He rolls his eyes, looking up to the rafters as if god himself would make her less frustrating. "Why did he come?"

Cause of course he's not letting her off so easily, and she has to squash her good mood in order to think about it clearly. "He wanted to give me a packet of papers. They're still outside." And the adrenaline and the terror threatens to wash over her again, and she can feel her eyes fill and her nostrils flare. "But it's good to talk to you," she says, and desperation tinges her voice exactly like she didn't want it to.

His face goes soft, and he gently, ever so gently, touches her hair, almost a light pet, a moment of such obvious comfort that the lump in her throat almost doubles in size.

"I'm okay, he didn't touch me, and my friend Trixie -- the one with the blond hair and the electrical wiring -- she dumped iced tea on him and he didn't do anything." She doesn't sound convincing, even to her self-serving and tricking ears. "Then he left when I pulled my gun on him outside, he didn't stick around and--"

His eyebrows flash up, right in front of her, but he continues stroking her hair.

"And he said Rey was out of prison." She finishes, the lump in her throat closing it out. She coughs, probably squeaking in an undignified manner, and Rodrick pulls her into something approaching a hug.

It's strange, in the way that they haven't hugged yet, and that he's only mostly solid most of the time, but she leans her forehead on the crook of his shoulder and sniffles for a few moments, as if that will help her feel better.

And it kinda does, in a way that she doesn't like to think of straight on, so after her eyes are under control and no longer leaking, she pulls back. "Why don't you want to speak?" She asks, cause anything besides this horror that's possibly waiting for her would be better.

He scowls at her and wrinkles his nose.

"It's fine, I can hear you fine, it's just like someone's whispering at you."

He shakes his head, then points to the laptop, as if that way of communicating is any better.

DIFFICULT.

And then,

FEELS RIDICULOUS.

A laugh bubbles up in her throat, cause after she's cried, any emotion is just easier and more immediate.

"It's not that ridiculous, I don't think so."

FEELS SO.

He gives her a long, appraising look, as if he can see through all her attempts to change the subject and not deal with this.

HE'S OUT OF PRISON?

"According to Mike he is. I don't...I don't think so." She leans back into the comfort of her new couch. "He'd already be here. He wouldn't send his flying monkeys to do the work when he could himself."

Rodrick weighs those words, deliberate.

TRICKING YOURSELF?

"That's rude," she mutters, staring at the screen.

PACKET OF PAPERS. LOOK?

And that would require her to go outside right now and confront the fact that Mike was there in the first place, so she doesn't move.

He tilts his head at her, eyes accusing, before he pokes her in the side again.

"I don't want to, okay? I'm only going to be upset by them." The words feel immediately too honest from her mouth, and she scowls at herself. "I try to, you know, not upset myself needlessly."

He opens his mouth as if to speak again, then shuts it again, poking instead at the computer.

COULD HAVE IMPORTANT INFORMATION. COULD HAVE DETAILS THAT YOU COULD USE.

And she knows that, but it doesn't help anything internally. "Fuck. Fine," she says, still feeling all the tears sitting in her sinus and in the back of her throat. Pushing herself up, she grabs her shotgun from the umbrella bucket, and hesitates before she unlocks the door. "Can you see me outside?"

He shakes his head.

"Like, at all?"

Again, he shrugs, then shakes his head.

"Fuck," she mumbles, and, feeling fragile, undoes the padlock and rolls up the door.

In the setting sun, no one is there, no cars, nothing. The air is still and cool, and she stalks over to the manila folder and snatches it up off the ground before all but running inside.

Rodrick gives her a relieved look the moment she comes in the door, and his shoulders relax as she re-padlocks it down.

She dumps the packet onto her overlarge table, as if that could possibly help dull whatever information is on the page and...sits at her table and looks at her phone instead.

Out of the corner of her eye she sees Rodrick throw up his hands in frustration.

But instead of looking at it, she pulls up her sister's number and hovers her hand over it, before deciding to text.

GRACE (5:22 PM): Mike showed up again. Said Rey was out of prison. Gave me a packet of papers and wants me to meet with Rey.

Immediately.

DEBORAH (5:22 PM): Don't.

GRACE (5:23 PM) I'm not stupid.

DEBORAH (5:23 PM) If any legal documents in packet, call me.

Deborah likes to consider herself a legal scholar, even though she dropped out of law school after three semesters. Still, she's probably a better analyst of it than Grace is, so...yeah.

She spreads the papers around without focusing on their contents, until they're all neatly laid out in a line on the long table, her eyes all but refusing to read the lines.

Rodrick leans forward on the pages, until his nose is almost touching them, standing halfway in the table. It's odd, especially now that she can touch him, to see him halfway into the furniture.

So instead of reading the packet she watches him, then flips on the lights when the sun finally sets.

After he's read -- or appeared to read -- all of them, he stands up straight and gives her an unreadable look.

"What," she says, defensive.

He points to the pages, still halfway bisected by the table, his face turning awfully gentle.

So she makes herself look. Forces her eyes to read and her pulse to calm down and her heart to stop thudding so damn hard.

It's...strange. Impersonal. A letter from a lawyer officially requesting her presence at a meeting, at an event of some sort, that's not clearly delineated. And the more she reads the letter, the more confused she gets.

"The law firm of Barnes and Bruegger formally request your presence for a seat at the table for the reading of a letter of intent, with the following people in attendance..." she reads out loud, as if reading out loud means she'll understand it more.

She doesn't.

She looks up at Rodrick, who shrugs, giving her a look as if it should be obvious.

GRACE (6:43 PM): Can you come over? It's a long letter and it is entirely in legal speak and it doesn't make sense.

DEBORAH (6:43 PM) I'm already halfway there. I started driving already.

GRACE (6:44 PM): Don't text and drive!

DEBORAH (6:45 PM): TOO LATE.

She sits back, locking eyes with Rodrick, who nods encouragingly.

"Could you make sense from this?"

He shakes his head.

"Yeah me neither."

DEBORAH COMES in and gives the door in the back of Grace's truck a dismissive glare.

"Assholes broke your door than gave you a legal document?" She snaps, shrugging off her jacket and dumping it on the couch with a bag.

Grace waves her hand at the pages spread out, and Deborah rolls her eyes before taking a look, gathering them up and taking them back to the couch.

It's awkward, as she reads, and Grace doesn't know what to do. It's like she's had too many emotions in one day, and now her little sister is here and she can't pull up the emotions to actually respond correctly.

All sneaky like, as if he thinks Deborah might be able to see him if he moves quickly, Rodrick sidles up to Grace, a soothing hand on her arm. Doing what she can to not, you know, appear super weird to be leaning on something invisible, she tilts her head to lean against his.

And it is weird, and she knows it's weird, but it's like having a secret support structure, something so secret even her family doesn't know what it is.

"Huh," Deborah says, once, then falls silent and reads the document again.

Grace sits, a bit of a distance away, on the sofa, knowing that she should be panicking even more than she currently is, and it's surreal. It's always surreal, when you're in a situation where the emotions should be higher than they currently are but you just can't give a damn.

After another two read-throughs, Deborah looks up to her older sister, her face scrunched up. "There's no legal requirement for you to show up, I think," she says, slow. "I think, I think it's more of an...official invitation for you to show up. So they can prove they tried."

"Prove they tried?" Grace tries to not be intrigued, of course, but that fails.

"Yeah, they had to show that they legally attempted to contact you for this," she says, pointing to a few lines. "They don't expect you to go at all, it's just a hurdle."

"What is it, though?" Grace asks, hating herself for asking. "What sort of meeting?"

"Could be anything from a court hearing, to a will reading, to some sort of charges." Deborah says, flipping through, then looking up at her sister with narrowed eyes. "They really don't want you there. They phrased this...look...deliberately obtusely."

Briefly, ever so briefly, Rodrick tightens his grip on her arm, before letting her go and just leaning against her.

"Why wouldn't they?" She asks before she can stop herself.

Because there are a myriad of reasons why they wouldn't want her at any legal proceedings. She could witness to any number of things, she could testify for court documents, she could inadvertently say something that could sink whatever he's building this time.

And, the small, unhealthy part of her, the part that is just yearning for revenge and to make them pay for making her so scared, is now raring to life to go to this.

Which Rey would know that about her. As if this is some sort of double gambit.

Deborah watches Grace as she comes to that realization and wilts into the couch. "Well, the quick answer is that it'd affect them to have you there and possibly able to say something in court that would affect the outcome," she says, matter of fact. "Or there could be some payout, some sort of thing you could gain or obtain from them, that they'd not want you to have."

"Or they could know I'd think that, and this is some sort of...I dunno...attempt to half convince me." Grace blurts out.

Deborah puts the papers down, a disappointed look appearing on her face, exactly the sort of look she used to inspire in her sister and family and exactly the sort of look she hates to get. "Grace," she starts, and her voice is an awful sort of gentle. "People don't do that."

"He does," Grace says, hating it, hating herself for saying that.

Deborah locks eyes with her for a long moment, then scoots over so she's pressed up against her sister's side. "Grace, you don't have to go back," she says, voice soft. "No one is thinking you're going to go back to him, no one wants you to, no one expects you to."

"Mom does," she points out, but that's a cheap shot. Mom wants her to go back because Rey was the man she lost her virginity to, and that sort of thing is important to her mother.

Deborah thins her lips. "And that's why we haven't told mom you live here, and we're not going to."

"Yeah."

Still, her sister snuggles up next to her, as if by sheer willpower she will comfort her sister. "The good thing is you're not legally obligated to show up," she says. "So...yay?"

Grace leans her head against her sister's, as if that will make it all better. "It'd almost be easier if I was."

Her sister hmmms, then falls silent, and they sit there.

Grace watches as Rodrick pushes himself up to his feet, and paces the length of the warehouse, pausing only at the grounded lamp to pass his hand through it, over and over again, like a moth to a flame.

DEBORAH LEAVES WAY LATE, and Grace gets herself very drunk on cheap wine while trying to read through the letters again.

But there's a reason she's a designer and a builder, for reading things like this isn't her strong point and never has been, so it's a mess of too large words and intentionally obtrusive sentences.

After probably an hour straight of wine and rereading, Rodrick stands over her, hands on his hips and eyebrows drawn together.

She stares up at him, and his face softens, before he pulls gently at her hand.

"I know, I know," she says, her mouth feeling like it's full of cotton and too many things. "I shouldn't..." she gestures at the pages, "obsess."

He nods, before he all but pulls her up. She doubts he actually could exert enough force to do so, but...yeah. She stands, and it's not like the world is unsteady, but she can feel her knees wobbling.

"It's just...he would play these mind tricks," she blurts, cause if her sister won't listen, then the ghost in her room might. "He would do this, he'd send something to intentionally discourage if they would be stubborn, then they would show up out of spite, and that's what he'd want."

Rodrick regards her with serious eyes, unblinking.

"He would play these manipulation games, and you just...couldn't know what he wanted, or if he really wanted you there or gone or..." She trails off, of course. "Yeah."

He stands there, with his hand in hers, before he softly, ever so softly pulls her in the direction of the staircase.

"What, you don't think I should sleep on the couch?" She mumbles.

He shakes his head, opens his mouth as if to speak, then shuts it.

A twist of something too close to pain hits her stomach, and she nods at him, oddly formal, before climbing the spiral staircase to her loft, keeping a grip on the bannister. He walks behind her, not as if he could catch her or anything, but the movement is nice, his hand on the small of her back.

In silence, she climbs into bed and he sits near her, and the overwhelming feeling that everything is falling apart overwhelms her as she sleeps.

10

She awakens on Saturday with no work, and four text messages, all from Heather.

HEATHER (6:02 AM): I need your expertise.

HEATHER (6:03 AM): And by expertise I mean your ability to see ghosts.

HEATHER (6:03 AM): And by ability to see ghosts, I know it's just the one ghost but I think I found another haunted area and I want to see if it transfers over to other ghosts.

HEATHER (9:51 AM): Are you awake? Was that too early to text?

She groans, her head throbbing a bit, before she swings her legs over the bed.

GRACE (10:19 AM): Sorry. What do you need?

On the floor below, Rodrick sits on the overstuffed chair, eyes unfocused and unmoving. It'd be creepy if she didn't see it so much.

HEATHER (10:20 AM): Can you drive to Riverside with me? You're halfway there and I can pick up, I got a tip on a haunted bookstore!

HEATHER (10:21 AM): Well, haunted book room in a thrift store.

Grace rubs her forehead, then pulls on a pair of jeans and stumbles downstairs.

GRACE (10:24 AM): Only if we stop by Starbucks.

WHEN SHE STEPS OUTSIDE of her warehouse to get into Heather's little mini car, Mike's sedan idles a few blocks away, just visible enough to be intimidating.

She breathes out hard through her nose, and gets into Heather's car anyways, accepting the coffee with something resembling joy. "Thanks," she says, and her throat sounds like she gargled with gravel. "Sorry for the late wake up."

Heather hands her a muffin as well, her eyes wide and excited, and she all but bounces in her seat. "My friend at the organization is sending me in cause she says I'm good with ghosts." She starts, immediately talking faster than reasonable for a Saturday morning. "And this is definitely a weird situation."

Grace takes a long sip of her coffee before facing her. "Organization?"

Heather flaps her hand at her, while driving. "It's a stuffy government thing? I don't pay much attention to it."

It sounds like a big deal, but the sort of big deal that's better after coffee. "So...Riverside?"

"Riverside." Heather drives, eyes bright in a way that Grace hasn't seen on anyone since about college. "Most of the time I get sent into these places and it's nothing, but the psychic who usually covers Riverside has a half confirmation so they're bringing me in. And I thought It might be good to see you in it as well, cause..." she merges seamlessly onto the freeway, and she's a surprisingly better driver than one would've thought. "Cause if you're already in the somewhat touching and okay at communicating phase, it's only a good thing."

"Yeah," Grace says, staring out the window in a hungover haze. "Oh, I can sorta hear him talk now."

If she was any bit less of a good driver, Grace has a feeling that Heather would've jerked the car. As it is, nothing. "Wow," Heather breathes, a smile on her face. "Does he talk a lot? Like a lot a lot?"

"Very little, actually." After all the conversation this week about Rey and personal safety and dark dramatic secrets, it's almost like this is a little mental break. "I think he's self conscious. He typed that it felt weird."

"I love that you type with him, I gotta recommend that to everyone," she says, still smiling so hard it looks like her face will freeze. "I've never heard of it, and it seems like just...the best thing to do. Did he have troubles accepting the technology?"

"Well he had been watching me use it for a few weeks, so not really." She drinks more of the coffee, and it starts dulling the pain in her head. "He likes it more than speaking."

Heather bobs her head in agreement as they drive. "I've never really heard of a shy ghost," she says, thoughtful. "Angry ones, yes, but not shy."

"Maybe you don't hear about them cause they don't cause the problems."

She shrugs, the smile still on her face.

~

RIVERSIDE'S already decked out in full Christmas gear, despite the fact that it's a) early November and b) over 85 degrees in the desert.

Heather drives her to the glisteningly beautiful downtown Riverside, with its adobe style buildings and mission style hotels, and they park a few streets away from the thrift store.

It's one of those multilevel thrift stores that you find in the more rural communities, with glass and dishes and old perfumes and rooms upon rooms of musty clothes.

"The book room is in the downstairs area, in the basement," Heather says, not looking at anything but what's in front of her as she walks briskly. Her hand is tucked into the ever present messenger bag.

"You doing that hand sensor thing?" Grace asks, following behind and feeling like a too tall child. The hangover is mostly gone, leaving behind just some weariness and the feeling that she needs way more water than she actually has consumed.

Heather nods, clattering down the stairs to the basement and pushing the door open. The door, Grace notes, that has a "DO NOT ENTER, DANGER" sign on it.

Inside, the room is musty and cold, colder than a basement should be, full to the brim with dimly lit metal bookshelves crammed full of books.

Grace immediately shivers, wrapping her arms around herself, the hair on the back of her neck sticking straight up.

"Woah," Heather mutters, eyes wide. "Okay, that's not fun. See anything?"

Grace peers between bookcases, but there's no dark figures or shadows on the wall. The shadows seem to climb around her, but it's the hangover and her eyes pulling tricks again, not anything actually happening. "I don't think so?" She shivers again. "It's cold though."

Heather shows her the hand sensor, and it's visibly buzzing in her hand. "Well, someone's here."

Grace nods, and the awful, skin crawling sensation of someone watching her bores down on top of her.

Heather takes a step and disappears behind one of the tall, tall bookcases. "Hello?" She says, tentative, and her voice echoes, in the cramped room. "Can you hear me?"

It's like bugs are trapped under the surface of her skin, and they crawl up around her. She shakes her hands out, but it does nothing to stop the feeling. "This doesn't feel okay," she calls out. But unlike Heather's voice, hers stops dead in its tracks, muted down into something resembling mush.

She stills, and phantom fingers grab at her arms and her throat. Not choking, they don't actually have the pressure...just grabbing.

"Heather?" She knows, she knows her voice isn't actually strangled, but it chokes out, small.

She can hear Heather shuffling around a few bookcases away, but she doesn't respond.

So Grace breathes out, hard, out of her nose, her pulse pounding.

For some reason, Rodrick had found her worthy of appearing to, or that he could appear in front of, so she squeezes her eyes shut and just...breathes for a second.

The fingers don't stop gripping and grabbing, moving along her arms and neck and back, poking and prodding.

She tries to move her feet, and it's like her feet are stuck in molasses.

Carefully, and the hands seem to follow when she does, she reaches to the nearest bookcase and raps her knuckles against it.

Heather's shuffling pauses, sudden. "Grace?" She calls out, and her voice echoes. "Grace was that you?"

The hand tightens briefly around her neck.

"Yes," she says, and her voice is a little louder. "Over here."

Heather turns the corner and stares at her, her eyes wide, before she tentatively approaches. "Is something happening?"

The hand grips down hard on her shoulder, so hard she would place money on it leaving bruises. And she knows how hard she can get gripped before it leaves bruises.

Heather stares at her, her eyes tracking down to the skin on her neck and arms, as if she can see the skin depress before her eyes. "Uh, Grace," she says, sticking the sensor back into her bag. "How about...How about you go back upstairs?"

"Yeah, good idea," Grace says, the hands still on her. She has no clue how many hands, cause, well, she can't see them, but it feels like way more than two.

She takes a step, faltering, and it's like moving through jelly, and...

A book flies off the bookcase, hitting the ground with a clatter.

She does her best not to flinch, cause flinches do no one good, but her heart pounds.

Another book clatters, as if the ghost is just throwing things to throw things, to stop her from leaving, to scare them.

"Stop," she says, forcing in all the authority she's never really been allowed to force out, and the hands still on her arm, gripping down hard. "Stop and let me go."

The hands soften for a moment, before one grabs her and tries to swing her around into the metal bookcase.

She stumbles, barely avoiding being swung around, but her stumble breaks the grip and she dashes towards the stairs.

The shadows lengthen, as if she is getting farther and farther away from the steps, but the moment her foot hits the step the pressure and the power it has over her vanishes, and she all but falls down on the steps.

The air is clearer, she can breathe easier, and the oppressive cold ends the moment she steps on the stairs. She sits down, hard, on the third step, keeping her toes from going over into the tip of the room.

Heather still stands in the middle of it, her eyes wide and stricken.

"Can you move?" Grace asks her, immediately gentling her voice. "It stops being able to touch you on the steps."

Heather nods, halting, and goes to her, sitting on the steps next to her, gingerly.

In the room below them, another book is hurled into the wall. They watch as it clatters and slides to the floor before it rests there, as if it had never been thrown.

"So yeah, some sort of haunting," Heather says, and her voice is quaking. "They...usually can't grab people. This one didn't say it could grab people. In the report. I wouldn't have brought you, at all, if it said that, that was weird, I've never actually seen that before and I've seen a lot of ghosts including unhappy ones and that doesn't make sense and..." She falls silent as another book flies across the room.

"Do you know how to calm it down?" Grace asks, feeling like Heather probably does but just got horrifically distracted.

Heather nods, slow. "I mean, probably? I have some." she grabs at her bag, then thinks for a moment. "There's an herb and witchcraft store like a block away, we can get stuff there."

An herb and witchcraft store seems a step too far on the belief scale, but as she lives with a ghost she shrugs and follows Heather back up the stairs.

She isn't kidding when she says a block away, and soon they're in a very fragrant and very tiny shop with Heather as Heather argues in a Slavic language with the store clerk over some sort of dried herbs.

The store is crammed full of crystals and cards and packets upon packets of dusty incense and ancient teas, and it smells roughly like an old foot.

Her skin tingles, especially where the ghost had gripped her in anger, the moment she steps into the room, and in a lull in the argument she waves over Heather. "Is there something here Rodrick would react well to?"

Heather thinks for a moment, nods, then resumes talking to the clerk in the Slavic language.

The clerk eyes Grace as if she is distasteful, but doesn't say anything direct except for adding a few crystals to the growing pile of things on Heather's purchase.

The moment that they step outside, Heather wrinkles her nose with a sigh. "They have good stuff there, but the guys a fucking creep," she mutters, her lip twisting up into probably the most distasteful look Grace has seen on her. "He didn't want to serve you because you had too much ghost residue on you."

"Ghosts leave residue?" Outside, in the dry desert winter heat, Grace is almost working up a sweat.

"Sorta. Some people can see it, apparently he's one of them."

"Think that's why the ghost in the basement there reacted like that?"

Heather heaves a sigh, her eyes narrowed in thought. "See, I think that that ghost probably has been trying to react like that to everyone he's come across, just you're the one who's been able to feel it? Ghosts don't just...try new things. They try the same movement over and over again until it works on someone."

"That's not quite true," Grace blurts out. "Rodrick...tries a lot of different things. To get his point across."

Heather seesaws, then nods. "Rodrick also has a person who's apparently sensitive living in his space for what, a month or two now? That changes how ghosts think, how they...process the world around them. I think." She shrugs. "At least according to all the existing research, he's acting like a normal un-problematic ghost with someone coexisting peacefully in his space. It's like old people." The turn is so sudden Grace blinks at her. "You know how old people, if left alone, sorta...lose their touch on a bunch of things? Have difficulties recalling and such?"

Grace nods, blinking rapidly.

"It's like that. Put someone in their space, make them interact, and they get a lot of things back. Start thinking again, like a person, and not like just a...remnant of a person."

They stand outside of the thrift store, the lights twinkling merrily in the window despite all the heat.

"So is that what you do?" Grace asks, as they stare at the glittering lights in the heat. "You go in and...make them remember?"

Heather chews on her bottom lip. "No? That's...really difficult to do. And time intensive. I just...I try to make it not be so confusing and...awful. You know?" She pats her now bulging messenger bag. "These mostly just...I dunno...soothe them? Make them not as outwardly angry. We don't..." she trails off, staring blankly. "We don't know exactly, but the ones we've been able to communicate with say it's nice. We don't know what, or why, or if existence hurts them and this is what helps, but they...seem to like it."

"Huh," Grace says, then, almost impulsively, opens the door for Heather to walk through. "Then let's make it less awful for that ghost?"

As they walk through, the owner gives them a wide eyed stare, as if utterly puzzled that they're going down there again, voluntarily.

On the staircase, Heather grabs Grace's hand and shoves a cloth wrapped satchel of herbs into it, and then another into the separate hand. "I don't know if he'll grab you when you're holding these, but they'll distract it, probably."

Grace grips them, and they crunch in her hands, giving off a sickly sweat herbaceous scent...something akin to the scent of a freshly broken stick of a sap filled wood, and takes a step off the stairs.

Again, immediately, the bookcases creak and the cold hits her like a slap. "Yeah, I know," she whispers, hoping somehow that she can be a force for soothing it yet again.

Heather disappears behind bookcases, deep into the room.

Fingers pry at her wrists and at her hands, so she loosens her grip on the bag, resting them in the palm of her hand. The fingers poke and prod at her hand, and she gets the very clear image that the ghost is trying to grab the sachet and is passing right through it.

"I know, I'm just going to put these on a few bookcases back here," she whispers, the hair on the back of her neck rising as she walks.

A hand strafes the back of her neck, then clamps down, hard enough to direct her but not hard enough to choke.

She gets to a fork in the bookshelves, and the hand directs her to go to the right. So she follows.

It gets progressively colder with each step, until she's in the darkest little corner, almost a little nook, where no bookcase stands, just some bare concrete and an ever so slight smell. A humid smell, the sort of smells you try not to think about too hard. The kinda smell that gives you the creeps, at some deep primal level, the kind of smell that makes you want to run away fast.

"Is this where you died?" She whispers, and the hand disappears from her neck and goes back trying to grab at her hands. One grabs her wrists and shakes her hand so hard she almost drops the sachet. "Oh, you want one here."

She places it gingerly on the ground, and the hand stops grabbing her.

She stares at the sachet on the ground, which remains undisturbed, but the hand no longer grabs at her. It's still bitterly cold, but...it's not touching her. So that's probably a plus.

Heather turns the corner and sees her standing there, and pales abruptly. "Grace?" She squeaks out.

Grace turns to her, and points at one of the sachets. "It directed me to put it down here," she says, and then takes a step out of the corner.

The hand fastens around her other hand with the remaining bag, and she gently puts it down right outside of the little corner.

Heather just stares at her, face slack.

"What?" She asks, feeling suddenly self conscious. "It just...sorta directed me, then it stopped when I put it down on the ground."

Something drips, hot, onto her shoulder and, against all her best judgement, she looks down.

A bright red spot of blood spreads on her white shirt, and, knowing it's stupid and knowing it would be better for her to do anything else but, she looks up.

A bright slightly spot of blood collates on the ceiling, dripping down, and she breathes hard out of her nose.

"Right."

Probably faster than is intelligent, she strides away and back to the stairs and, nothing stops her.

AFTER BUYING an ill designed shirt from the very grateful thrift store and throwing her old one in the trash, Heather has a long discussion with the store owner about how they have to leave the sachets down there but, for the love of god, send a cleaner. Grace sits on one of their old couches, by the sunny window, trying desperately to warm herself up in the sunbeam.

"It's not actual blood," Heather remarks to her, casually. "It's just a manifestation of the blood in what was probably a very messy killing."

That doesn't help, but Grace follows Heather outside, to the heat that almost banishes the chill. "Well, they seemed to like it when I put down the sachet. When I was walking there, I think it was trying to grab at it, but just went right through it."

Heather nods as she unlocks her car. "Well, I got an extra one for Rodrick, we'll see how he likes it."

"Or at least get his opinion on it," she says, her skin still crawling. "He didn't like your buzzer thingie."

WHEN HEATHER DROPS HER OFF, Mike's idling car is nowhere to be seen and her door is still thankfully intact, and the doorbell never buzzed her phone, so she unlocks and rolls up the interior door.

From across the large room, where he sits curled up on the over-stuffed chair, Rodrick's head shoots up.

He stares at her, eyes wide, before he slowly and deliberately pushes himself up off the chair and stalks over.

"Did anyone try to get in?" She asks, after rolling in her truck.

He stares at her, and it's not a nice look.

"I saw Mike's car outside when I left, did he try to get in?"

He slowly shakes his head, his eyes narrowing, and he reaches a tentative hand to the back of her neck...right where the ghost had gripped her to direct her.

"Yeah, encountered another ghost today, he -- or she I guess -- wasn't super nice." His hand trails down her arm, where the probable bruises are hid by her long sleeves. "Heather took me with her to see how powerful the ghost was."

Rodrick's eyes narrow to slits, and he gently picks up her hand, where the ghost gripped her when trying to grab the bag of herbs. He opens his mouth, closes it, then opens again. "They touched you." His voice is flat, even accounting for the distant sound and the distortion. "You let them touch you."

"Wasn't really my choice, I walked in and it was grabby." Something in his tone prickles at the back of her throat, something too controlling and too familiar. "We pretty much immediately left to get some bags of shit from a store, then brought the stuff back. It stopped after it showed me where to put it."

His mouth thins, and he pokes her, gently, where the drop of blood had dripped on her shirt.

"Yeah, it apparently...manifested blood and dripped on me. It was gross."

Rodrick gives her a deeply disappointed look, then, holding her hand like it will break, pulls her onto the couch and into something that at least resembles cuddles.

"Are you okay?" She asks, the prickly feeling moving into confusion.

He wraps his arms around her, and almost out of necessity she leans her head against his shoulder, and he's satisfyingly solid.

"You just spoke so I know you can do it, are you okay?"

He makes a noise in the back of his throat, deep, and she blinks rapidly.

"Are you...jealous that I saw another ghost?" She asks, the prickly feeling back in her throat. "I mean, I didn't mean to be grabbed?" Her voice is small, much smaller than she wants it to be, and she closes her eyes as she thinks up a curse.

"Yes?" He speaks, soft. "But no?" He puts a hand on her hair, moving it idly. "Other ghost shouldn't have grabbed you. That's...rude."

She takes a second before she speaks again, because she knows where her mind is going and she also knows that she shouldn't assume that of everyone she's around, because not everyone is a jealous asshole and she shouldn't expect them to be.

"Rude?"

His chest moves up and down, as if he sighs, as if he still needs to draw air. "It's like they didn't like that you had seen me, and wanted to...smear the fact that they touched you all over. It's rude." It might be the most words he's spoken to her at one time, and it's about ghost politics. "It's not a territory thing, but it's rude."

Again, she takes the moment to think, so she doesn't blurt out the emotionally unhealthy option that's at the tip of her tongue. "Rude of me or of the other ghost?"

"The ghost." He speaks, soft, but even though it's soft it's still perfectly audible, and the thought gives her a little bit of the warm fuzzies deep in her chest. "It is clear that you have seen me, and inter-acted with me, and then it...what, just grabbed you?" His voice is clearly, clearly offended, and she wishes they had had this conversa-tion about anything else. "That's rude, right? It feels rude."

"Is this like dogs who don't like when you've been sniffed at by other dogs?"

He sighs, wearily. "Did you compare me to a dog?"

And yes she did, but also she doesn't want him to stop talking because this is excellent. "It's a metaphor."

He's silent, just his arms wrapped around her, and it's the most cuddling she's gotten from a non-family member in ages, and she can't help but close her eyes and enjoy it.

"So yes, it is like that," he says, his voice deep and begrudging. "It's rude and that other ghost should've been nicer and not, you know, grabbed you like that."

"It was rude and I think they tried to swing me into a bookcase."

He straightens, and the cuddling moment is broken and she sits up as well. "They tried to hurt you." He says, flat.

"It was not a nice ghost. Calmed down with the herbs, though. Really liked those."

"It tried to hurt you," he repeats, and his face is as icy cold as it was when he exploded the lightbulb. "The psychic with the buzzer took you there?"

She nods, and he scowls. "She sent me back with some of the herbs, saying that ghosts usually like them?"

He gives her the flat stare, then twists away and vanishes.

She stares at the place where he just was, and tentatively puts her hand out. Nothing. "I'll bring that in later, how about?" She says, then pushes herself up to change and shower away any possible weird ghost residue.

AFTER A FEW HOURS OF SILENCE, Rodrick reappears when she opens her truck door and pulls out the sachet that Heather had crafted for him.

He gives it a narrowed eye look, the look she internally calls the skeptical look.

"This is what we placed in the room to help the other ghost."

He rolls his eyes at the mention of the ghost, but peers closely at the sachet.

"Heather says that ghosts tend to like this, but she doesn't know why. Says it calms down unhappy and violent ghosts." She pauses, then powers on. "If you don't like it or if it sedates you or does something against your will please tell me because all my instincts on this are that it's sketchy and I don't like the idea of making someone calm against their will."

He raises an eyebrow at her, then nods, as if begrudgingly impressed.

"I know that the other ghost--" there's the immediate eye narrow -- "really wanted them placed where it had died, in a corner of a bookstore. Do you want that?" She points to where the overstuffed chair is.

He steps up, and cradles her hand with the sachet in it, and opens his mouth as if to speak, then shuts it abruptly, his eyes wide.

"Does it...does it stop you from speaking?"

He nods, abrupt, and she tosses it back in the truck.

"Okay then, that'll stay there."

His mouth twists, decidedly unhappy.

She shuts the truck door again, and he drifts to her laptop, casting the 'follow me' eyes back at her.

"Did it stop you permanently cause I can throw it away outside."

He shakes his head, but still points to the laptop.

She sighs, opening it anyways. "I like your voice, I don't want you to stop using it."

He pokes at the keys, slowly.

WHEN I SPEAK I FORGET I DIED.

She sits back, spine crawling at that. "That's...dark."

He nods, leaning against her as he types through her.

THAT THING SMELLED NICE BUT I DIDN'T LIKE IT. IT MADE ME FEEL LIKE SOMETHING WAS MISSING.

She nods, leaning against him back. He makes a noise deep in his chest, a strange noise, one that both sends a thrill down her spine and terrifies her. "Well, sorry for the confusion, I'll let Heather know what it does for you."

His nose wrinkles up, as it does with most mentions of the psychic.

"She said you're pretty remarkable." Grace says, sudden, on impulse. "Said that you're reacting pretty much exactly like you should with me living here."

He rolls his eyes, types.

GLAD TO GET A REPORT CARD.

"They had report cards in the 1930s?"

THIS WAS A WAREHOUSE AFTER THAT, TOO. PEOPLE TALK ABOUT FAMILIES, I PICK UP ON THINGS.

She nods against him, feeling like she should say more but not knowing what to say.

He seems struck by the same impulse, and he cuddles up against her, almost distressed, and they stay like that for a few hours, until she drifts off to sleep, pillowed against his shoulder.

WHEN SHE WAKES UP, dawn is cracking its way through her high vaulted windows, and she's curled up on the couch, alone, and something resembling a pang goes through her.

Still, she stretches out, staring up at the steel beam ceiling high above her, as the light turns from a dark blue to a light pink inside this strange home she's created.

After the light is suitably yellow and firmly into daylight, she puts her feet on the ground, fixing herself breakfast and a coffee and starting to run epoxy over her nice work table.

It's the perfect mindless work, the sort of work she prefers, where she doesn't have to think or focus or occupy her mind with anything, and she lets her mind wander.

For most of her career, her mind has wandered directly to Rey. First in the infatuated way, in the way that most people's minds wander to the one they're in love with, but then, slowly, ever so slowly, in the way that is underlined with quiet foreboding. The focus on having to make someone happy, to the disappointment of making a mistake, to the slow evolution of terror when the person shows their true colors.

And his true colors didn't come out quickly, or, if they did, they came out when she was so deep into the pool of infatuation and first love that she ignored them, she didn't register them as threats.

And now, as she runs a coat of epoxy over the table and fiddles with the brackets holding up the reinforced legs, her thoughts of him are mostly of planning, of conniving.

She's gotten away from him before, with less, and she can keep him away. Even if, like Mike claims, he's out of prison.

If nothing else, she can shoot her own goddamn shotgun, and she couldn't do that before.

As if sensing her thoughts, Rodrick flickers into existence near the table, giving it his standard skeptical and curious look.

"I'm making it so I can do detail work without having to worry about the quality of the wood of my bench," she says, almost on autopilot.

Most people who epoxy wood like this don't do construction, but detail work, like jewelry or some other time intensive work. People doing construction generally don't like epoxy because it can dent or scratch too easily, but she prefers it. Likes the ability to see the motions and the places she impacts.

Her therapist would call it control issues and the need to prove that her actions have real consequences, but Grace calls it personal and professional taste.

Rodrick doesn't react either way, but dips his hand through the table in a way that's truly disorienting.

Something is on his mind, somehow, and she can see the furrow of thought in his brow.

"Everything okay?"

He opens his mouth, pauses, then goes forward with speaking. "You asked, yesterday, if anyone had tried to get in." His voice is faltering, as if he is unsure of what to say.

She nods, her lips thinning, and tightens the bracket underneath the center of the lip. "He was waiting in his car when I left with Heather, and he didn't follow."

He looks down, his lips twisting. "When I'm not...here, or interacting, or actively thinking, I don't...I don't track time well. At all. I'm...I'm not sure I was conscious the entire day."

She straightens and looks at him, and he avoids her glance. "What, like you were napping?"

He shrugs, and she gets the feeling that it's a very incomplete metaphor. "Somewhat?"

She nods at him. "I mean, that's fine, I'm not asking you to be awake the entire time you're here, that's kinda cruel."

Relief breaks over his face, like she's granted something far kinder than just permission to be the way he is. "I'm saying I don't know if someone tried to get in." He grits out, moving his hand in and out of the still wet epoxy with no consequence. "I can't always know these things. No one got in, but I don't know if they tried."

And that makes sense, it truly does, and she feels like she's missing something in how she should be reacting right now. "I was just asking, I'm not demanding."

"But you're not safe, and you need to be safe, and I couldn't say that you were." He bursts out, before clamping his mouth shut.

She sets down her wrench, sitting back on her heels and pushing the sweaty hair out of her eyes, at a loss for words.

Her therapist had warned her, several times, that people might react with inappropriate amounts of worry, but she hadn't actually gotten an idea of how to deal with it when it came to.

"Rodrick, you're not responsible for my safety?" She says, and hates how her voice tilts up at the end. "I mean it's very nice but no one person can be responsible for that sort of thing. I'm barely responsible for that sort of thing."

His lips twist again.

"If anything, having you here increased my safety?" Again, her voice sounds way more unsure than she actually is. "I mean, you certainly don't hurt it, and you had the ideas with the cameras."

He nods, begrudging, as if wanting to say something controversial but, at the same time, desperately not wanting to talk about it. "Before..." He gestures, vague. "When they tried to sell this place, before you but after the factory, someone thought about buying, set up sensors. They're gone now, but would that help?"

She's not going to tell him that there were about 35 years between her buying it and the factory, but his point still stands. "Like motion sensors? Would you set those off?"

Again, the skeptical. "I don't...I didn't then?"

"But they could help with alerting things."

"And if you placed them on the building outside, along the foundation, maybe?"

She nods along with him, a thought pushing at the back of her mind. "Is there...a sort of thing you could impact?" She asks, picking up the wrench again and tightening another bracket. "Like something we can put in that you could influence and set off in case there's anything you think I should see?"

His eyes light up. "Sometimes, wire."

"So if I run an electrical current through something, I could possibly..." She pulls out her phone, flips it to the notes app and starts tapping things out. "I could maybe hook it up to something that sends an auto text if you trip it."

He gives her a smile, a shy smile, one that makes her bashful in response, makes her feel incredibly lucky that she got this ghost and not the angry ghost of that bookstore.

"I think I could hook that up, that's even easier to rig than most of the lighting and internet I got up here. It'd have to be along a wall, so I wouldn't trip over it or anything, cause I'd do that."

He nods, falling silent again, but his shoulders are down and his face is relaxed, and he just watches her as she finishes tightening the brackets and sockets the work table back into place.

OBTAINING the supplies for that is as easy as buying some copper wiring at the local Home Depot, some sensors that can be Wi-Fi controlled, and a few long lasting batteries, and it feels way too easy.

But Rodrick patiently waits for her to set up a trial bit, then practices running his hand down it, which does in fact create an electrical blip, the barest of interruptions in the flow of the electrical current, and she fiddles with the sensor until it's able to take care of it, to pick up on it enough so that it knows to send her a text.

"I'm gonna have to ask you to never walk through someone who's wearing a pacemaker," she jokes, and then has to explain pacemakers to a rather confused ghost who died in the 1930s and therefore way before any of that technology was around. Which involved a fair amount of Googling and Wikipedia reading and then he got excited about Wikipedia and she spends a few hours switching from page to page as he reads about the most truly random things.

It's almost homey, and it's almost cozy, and it's just enough like an actual friendship and relationship that it sends all those messed up warning signs up and down her spine.

11

Her next workday is a solo workday, just her building up the support structures for the lighting system they built into that one Beverly Hills house. It's easy work, the sort of work that's filled with sawdust and nails and deep satisfaction afterwards.

After she has what is fundamentally a nice wooden box built, sanded, primed, and painted, and in the approximate spot so she can come back to it the next day for finishing, she steps outside to see Mike and a few nameless goons waiting for her by her truck.

She's covered with sawdust and paint, and her hair is pulled back into a sweaty braid, but the two nameless goons gaze at her with something akin to fear.

"I won't go with you," she calls to Mike, digging out her keys from her purse, her heart pounding. She really doesn't want to shoot someone in front of a job site, but her shotgun is there nonetheless and is probably a good idea to get into her hands as soon as possible.

The goons look at each other, and she tries to remember if they were there when she was there, but she draws a blank. Most of the faces blurred together during her time there, and these ones are even more generic Irish men than normal.

"He's going to find you, and it's going to be better if you go to him on your own terms," Mike says, as if he is trying to figure out how to say what he needs to say in the most foreboding terms possible.

She actually finds herself rolling her eyes, before she faces them. Both the goons blanche. "If he wanted to find me, he wouldn't be sending you, we both know that, right?" Her voice quivers, just a little bit, and she hates herself for it.

Mike glances at the two goons, before he nods at them, and they both get into the comically tiny sedan. Everyone seems far too large for that tiny of a car.

Once the door closes, he slumps a bit, but she's not fooled by it. "Come back, it'll be so much better. For you, for everyone."

The hair on the back of her neck raises. "I'm not going back to him, not now, not ever," she says, parroting the words her therapist suggests she use whenever she has that impulse.

He stares at her, blue eyes wide. "He's a nightmare right now," he says, slow. "He's a nightmare and just demands you back, but doesn't want to come and beg.

"Good, I don't want to see him."

Internally, deep inside, she quakes, in the way that everyone wants to know they're wanted, the deep down moment where you just know that they are worse off without you, and that part that makes you want to come back to remedy it immediately.

Mike's nostrils flair, and he -- probably unconsciously -- flexes his shoulders, and she's immediately reminded that he's so much bigger than her. "We can drag you back," he warns.

She knows this, and knows it's always been an option. "I go missing, I have people who know where to look," she bluffs, opening her truck and sliding in her seat, pulling the shotgun onto her lap and pointing it at his direction.

He stares at her, his jaw working.

"And we both know he's going to be very unhappy if you hurt me."

"Will you at least go to the legal counsel?" He asks, almost desperate, and it strikes her as wrong and incomplete. The pieces don't add up.

"What's important at the legal counsel?" She gestures with the shotgun, and his eyes immediately flicker to it, then to the car where the goons are waiting. "The letter was pretty unclear."

She can see the cogs working behind Mike's eyes. "He wants to offer you money," he says, after a long break.

She raises an eyebrow at him. "Right," she says, because getting into debt with a man like Rey seems like a great idea. "Well, not gonna go."

She reaches over her shotgun, and closes her truck door in his face, before peeling out and away.

By the time she gets to the first major intersection, the giant Beverly/Crescent/Sunset clusterfuck, the sedan idles up behind her, and her heart jumps again.

Hands fumbling, she pulls out her phone and dials her sister on speed dial.

"Gracie?" Her sister's voice is tinny.

"Mike showed up at my work, they're following me now, I'm in Beverly Hills." She blurts out, quick, then takes a deep, shuddering breath. "They said they want to offer me money to return."

"Don't." Her sister's voice is flat, even for the phone.

"I know, I know, they...they said he needs me." Her voice breaks again.

"One sec." Her sister pulls away from the phone, says something muffled, then comes back, "Are you going home? Can you call a friend to stay?"

Her mind immediately flashes over to Rodrick, and the inevitable panic he would have with what's going on. "I think so, yeah."

"Good, call them, I'm in Kansas right now," Deborah says, firm. "I'd be there, but I'm too long of a plane flight away."

Grace nods, her hands shaking and her eyes filling with tears, which is not productive to driving, so she pulls over into that giant under construction Beverly Hills mall, and can't tell if the sedan pulls into the parking garage with her.

So, covered in sawdust and paint and sweat, she browses in a bunch of too expensive stores, trying to get her hands to stop shaking, when her phone beeps.

HEATHER PSYCHIC (6:21 PM): How'd he like the herbs?

It's such a break from what she's dealing with that she takes a big gasp of air, as she's browsing in the Sephora. The clerk gives her a side eyed look.

GRACE (6:23 PM): He hated it and it made it so he couldn't talk, so I threw it away.

She gets the sudden, strong impulse that she really wants to see Rodrick, to be back in her little safe place in the warehouse with him, and be able to think about the metaphysical ramifications of having a dead person for a roommate instead of this shit with Rey.

HEATHER PSYCHIC (6:25 PM): Really??????? Strange!!!!!! He might like incense, then, cause that increases stuff instead of the herbs. Those decrease.

And that does make sense, but she stares hard at her phone, breathing through her nose.

HEATHER PSYCHIC (6:29 PM): Like how weed slows a person down. But cocaine speeds them up.

GRACE (6:29 PM): Did you try to give my ghost weed?

HEATHER PSYCHIC (6:30 PM): It's a metaphor.

And that's besides the point, but a bubble of inappropriate laughter floats up in her chest, chasing away the vague panic gripping her there.

WHEN SHE PULLS into the abandoned warehouse district, there's no other cars, and she refuses to feel grateful for that fact. They know where she lives, they know she knows, so them not showing up is as clear a message as them doing so.

The moment she rolls up the interior door and pulls her truck in, Rodrick flickers into being, giving her a curious look.

"You're bothered," he speaks, and his words are the clearest she's heard so far.

She shuts the truck door, and he follows her up her stairs to the loft, where she sheds the sawdust infused clothes in exchange for her pajamas. "Got followed at work again, I'm exhausted by it," she says, feeling like she needs to ramble. "They tried to offer me money to come back." She flops onto the bed, like the strings have been cut off of her.

He sits, folded up, on the floor next to the bed.

"I mean, it makes no sense." She's staring up at the ceiling, at the steel beams running along the length of it. "They know how I feel. They have it in court documents how I feel. I'm not some...someone who goes back, just because he's claiming to miss me."

She might've been, at one point, but not after everything that happened, not after the crappy little apartment and reclaiming herself bit by bit after she escaped.

Rodrick doesn't speak, just rests his head on his arms, sitting with his knees pulled up to his chest.

"It's insulting." She tries out the words, slowly. "It's insulting that they think I would."

"Why would they?" He whispers, but his voice isn't full of judgement, just soft wonder.

She takes a deep breath, staring at the ceiling still, as if that will make this conversation easier, as if thinking about this with another person is normal. "I think...I think they thought I'd be a pushover," she says, "I mean, I was. At one point, when I was with him. It's survival, not anything else."

"Survival?"

She turns her head to look at him, and he's watching her, avid, like someone would look at the surface if they were drowning. "You caved, or he got upset. It became..." She knows her therapist gave her much more adept words at dealing with this, but they're not coming to mind right now. "It became a way to guarantee you wouldn't have a bad day."

The skin around Rodrick's eyes tighten, and he sits up, closer, his face blank. "sThings might've...changed...since me." he says, as if he's choosing his words with equal care, "but if I saw a man doing that to a woman, me and my pals would break his head in."

"Yeah, that's still a thing, but..." She cracks a smile at him. He doesn't smile back. "Just he had way more friends than I did."

His lips thin, but the blank look doesn't fade. "If I saw a friend of mine do that, he'd quickly have no girl and no friends."

And she knows that abuse like that happened aplenty in the 1930s, but it's heartwarming nonetheless. "Thanks," she says, and it feels inadequate.

He nods, and she rests a hand on his shoulder, and he feels solid under her touch. A shudder moves through him, like a shock, and he reaches and places his own hand over hers.

"I don't know what it's like to be you," she blurts out, in the too soft moment, when it stretches on too long. "But I'm kinda glad you're here."

A look spasms over his face, quick and pained, and he grips her hand tighter, before gentling. "You can shoot him?" He suggests, his voice forcefully cheerful. "Death's not too bad, it'll get him out of your way."

She blinks at him, then rolls back onto her back and laughs, and he chuckles with her.

THE NEXT MORNING he spends it, blank, curled up on the overstuffed chair, in the spot that no longer feels cold to Grace, and somehow it doesn't feel as foreboding as it did the first time she saw him that way.

She doesn't know if he's pondering being dead, or reliving his own death, or if that's just a comfortable spot for him, so she ignores him until her doorbell rings, loud.

He doesn't move at the sound, so she puts down her sander and grabs at her phone, booting up the app.

Whoever it is stands too close to the doorbell for her camera to pick up on their face, so she sees mostly just upper torso. Heart pounding, sudden, she flicks open the app for the speaker. "Who's there?"

There's a grunt, but nothing else. So, someone masculine, who thought they would just get her to open up the door but not tell her who it is.

"If you don't say who it is I won't answer the door," she says, and her voice quakes.

As if slowly waking up, Rodrick blinks, raising his head towards the sound of her words.

Grace's heart pounds, and the doorbell rings again.

She locks eyes with Rodrick, who lets his gaze slide to the shotgun in the umbrella bucket.

"Yeah, good idea," she says, stalking over, her hands shaking.

He follows behind, face serious but still somewhat peaceful, as if he just awoke from a deep nap.

Carefully, ever so carefully, she rolls up the interior door, happy to find her new exterior door still nicely locked. "Who is it?" She calls out.

A muttered noise, nothing clear and concise at all.

Heart pounding, she closes her eyes and counts to three, then swings open the door, the shotgun in her hand and —

Comes face to face with a very surprised delivery man, whose eyes drop immediately to the shotgun, then snap up to her face.

"Oh," she says, then fits the shotgun back into the umbrella basket. "Um."

He stares at her, face slack, before extending his arm out with a small box. "De-livery?" He stutters out, through a very thick accent, the white of his eyes visible around his irises.

"I'm so sorry." Grace breathes, her face heating up, because of course it's something innocent and of course she just majorly overreacted and scared the shit out of some perfectly innocent delivery guy. "I'm so sorry, I have a stalker, I just can't risk it, I'm so sorry."

He blinks at her, obviously not understanding a word she says.

So she signs for the package and takes it inside, rolling down the door behind herself.

"It was just a fucking delivery guy," she mutters.

Rodrick slides up beside her as she puts the box on the table. "Why didn't he answer?" His voice is grumpy, even beyond the normal 'just woke up' impulse.

"I don't think he spoke the language well," she says, trying hard and probably failing to not sound bitter. Just another situation where she thought the worst and it turns out she was actually fine, and it leaves a shitty taste in her mouth.

So instead of dwelling on that, she pulls her box cutter out of her pocket and slices open the box, which is the bracket fixer she bought about a week ago and forgot was on its way. Because that is her life now.

But with the bracket fixer, she can get the actual cube bookcase installed, just has to schedule that to happen.

Rodrick stares at it, then at her, eyebrows together. "Do...people not need to know English to get jobs?" He asks, tentative, as if he thinks it's a risky question.

She really doesn't want to explain this to him, especially cause he was last alive with Ellis Island as a big part of the American immigration control center. "Well, for a lot of jobs, yes, but...not every job. And it's usually rooted in some sort of racism or anti immigration or something like that."

His face screws up. "Why would America be anti immigration?" Which is an adorable thing for a white man to say, but she doesn't really have the presence of mind to explain.

"Well, weren't they anti Irish when you were alive?"

He shakes his head, then thinks, then nods.

"Exactly."

She sets the bracket fixer on the table, then stares down at it, before picking up her computer and scheduling the delivery of the bookcase wall.

"This next part, this weekend, there will be a lot of people coming in and out," she says, closing the laptop and looking up at Rodrick, where he stands halfway in and out of the tabletop, just watching her curiously.

Sometimes she forgets that he's a ghost, and then he goes and stands in her furniture.

He looks, obviously, at the door.

"I'll ask my sister and my work friend to come as well? So they can make sure no one walks in when they're moving in furniture?" She guesses.

He nods, settling into the couch next to her, where she would love to stay but now her heart is pounding and some time today she needs to make her way over to Beverly Hills and finish the box. The box that she's really being paid way too much money to build, for what it is, but Beverly Hills pays Beverly Hills prices.

She heaves a sigh, then another, then puts the laptop down. "Well, I'm awake now. That was a bit too much adrenaline for..." She checks her cell phone. "For 9:30 on a Wednesday. Who delivers at 9:30, anyways?"

Rodrick shrugs. "The whole delivery thing is weird to me in the first place," he mumbles, voice again far away. "Feels like bad science fiction."

"I've shown you the internet, with Wikipedia, and Netflix, and delivery is bad science fiction?"

"The internet is good science fiction, it's the buying things from it and having it come to your door that's bad science fiction."

She pauses, then opens up her laptop again. "Has, somehow, anyone shown you Star Wars?"

He raises an eyebrow, and she starts to play A New Hope.

TRIXIE IS BACK, and does miscellaneous wiring work in the ceiling panels as Grace finishes the very official box and installs it.

For being what is essentially a plain wooden box, she is getting way too much money for it, but it blends with the decor of the room while hiding the blatant electrical stuff, which was the priority.

After climbing down the ladder, Trixie nods at the box, smirking. "Nice."

Grace shrugs, cause they have all been asked to do ridiculous things in the name of interior decorating jobs. "You busy on Saturday?" She asks, sudden, because being able to ask it quickly is always better.

Trixie shrugs, then thinks. "I have to pick up my friend from the airport at like 11P PM?"

"I'm gonna be putting in that giant wall, I could use your electrical knowledge to make sure the lights don't look janky," she says, then pauses. "And there's gonna be a lot of contractors and people I don't know, so....having someone else there would be great."

Trixie raises her eyebrows for a second before she comprehends it. "Ohhhh I see," she says.

"I'll let you look at the wiring I've been doing on the loft--it's probably a mess to your standards."

"Sure," she says, overly casual, like Grace wasn't asking for something that could be a big deal. "They still bothering you?"

She nods towards outside. "They were here when I left after building yesterday," Grace says, and this time her voice doesn't quaver. "They want me to show up to some sort of legal proceedings, and think that intimidating me is the way to do it."

Granted, they are very intimidating and even Grace just a year ago would probably have caved and caved hard.

Trixie wrinkles her nose. "Isn't that a good way to guarantee you don't show up?"

"Yeah that's the secondary theory, it's pretty confusing."

THAT NIGHT, Rodrick is nowhere to be seen, so she crashes in her bed super early and reads on her phone instead of doing normal adult things like cleaning or making dinner.

Later, after she's fallen asleep and woken up and fallen asleep a few times with her phone in her face, she gets drawn up to consciousness by something...vague. The sort of wakening that alerts the brain, but the senses don't immediately draw on something that could have caused the wakefulness.

She blinks her eyes open, and in the dim light from the street lamps outside, she can barely make out the dim form of Rodrick sitting on the far edge of her bed.

Her heart jumps, just a little, before she calms herself intentionally. "You scared me," she whispers, cause it's the wee hours of the morning and it feels too raw to speak at full volume.

His eyes search her face, unreadable, for a few seconds. "Thought you were asleep." His voice is far away, like being called out from a great distance.

It's a strange thing, his voice. Sometimes it's a far away echo, sometimes it's immediate, like he is right there next to her, and she hasn't quite put into patterns what it sounds like and when. Something to do with mood, something to do with how much she's been around him, and something to do with something else, something she hasn't quite put a finger on.

He cocks his head at her, and she tries a smile. "Are you okay?" Cause he has always been pretty much a cartoon caricature of gentlemanly behavior, especially when it comes to her getting changed or her on her bed, so sitting directly on it feels...odd. Like something would have to propel him to do something like this, even if she is okay with it.

It's also something they've never spoken of, and something she is a bit grateful she doesn't have to do anything about. Because cuddling on a couch is nice without having to say it ends there.

His eyes cast down, and he moves his hand idly through the comforter.

"Is someone outside?" She asks, the hair on the back of her neck raising. "Did someone try to get in?"

He shakes his head, quick, before frowning thoughtfully. "I didn't mean to wake you."

It's in the same sort of tone that he's said things in before, and she privately puts it in his category of things that he says when he doesn't mean to have an effect but privately hoped he'd have the effect. For someone who spends half his time nonverbal, he gives off a lot of those vibes.

She sits up, reaches to him and places a hand on his arm. His skin -- or whatever pseudo spiritual part of him she's touching that approximates his skin -- is cool to the touch, the temperature of the air around her. She hasn't felt overly cold with him for a while now.

His eyes fall to her hand, as if each time she touches him is still a shock. Quick as a flash, his eyes dart back up to hers.

"You okay?" She asks, again, the moment feeling still unreal, like the dawn hour coats it in some sort of surreal wash.

Granted, she's asking the question of a ghost, in the abandoned warehouse in which she now lives, but still.

His lips twist, and he nods, slow, reluctant. "I have nothing wrong,"

She punches the blankets around her legs, the last bit of sleep chasing its way out of her brain, and checks the time. 5 AM, so right before dawn, so it's not a wasted time to wake up, just slightly inconvenient. "So what's up? You don't generally come up here to wake me up if there's nothing wrong."

Again, his face twists in something resembling dissatisfaction, and it's suddenly awkward.

"Do you...not know what's bothering you?" She guesses, and relief crashes over his face.

She props up the pillows behind herself, blinking the sleep out of her eyes.

"So...something is bothering you, you don't know what exactly, and you thought you'd wait for me to wake up," she says, and her voice sounds flat and rough to her ears. "Is it just boredom?"

He shakes his head, and now he looks embarrassed, and she gets the sudden feeling that he is really regretting coming up to speak to her, that there is a nebulous need that he's confused by and now, when asked to explain it, he can't put it to words.

She feels that there's a lot of things like this, where he spent so long having all these emotions and needs that now that he has an opportunity to speak about them, they're knotted up into a ball in his chest, leaving him unable.

The loneliness of that is unbearable, so she rubs his arm, hoping to be soothing, and he leans into her touch. "It's alright, if you can't really figure it out," she says, repeating words her therapist said to her many times.

He gives her a sharp look, something unreadable, before he leans in, pressing his cool lips gently to hers.

She freezes at the unfamiliar touch, and he immediately draws back, eyes wide, and they stare at each other for a few beats, before he disappears.

She blinks at the space where he used to be, then cranes her neck to see if he appeared anywhere downstairs, but nothing.

"That's not fair for you to do something like that and then disappear!" She calls out, out of a fit of something resembling both amusement and anger. "I can't disappear, it's not fair."

Of course, there is no response, so she flops down on the bed again, pressing the heels of her hands to her eyes in frustration, as the room slowly starts to get streaked with pink light.

12

She's not sure if he's embarrassed or if he's afraid, but he doesn't show himself for the rest of the morning, as she gets up and crafts herself some breakfast and coffee.

GRACE (7:14 AM): So Rodrick kissed me last night.

HEATHER PSYCHIC (7:14 AM): Um.

GRACE (7:15 AM): Is there anything I need to be aware of? Or do?

HEATHER PSYCHIC (7:16 AM): I'll check but I dunno.

LATER, while adding on a molding to the edges of the box, her phone beeps again.

HEATHER PSYCHIC (10:41 AM): Did he say anything about why he kissed you? Or anything like that?

Grace wipes off the wood glue onto her jeans before tapping out a reply back.

GRACE (10:42 AM): He disappeared pretty much immediately. I think he was embarrassed.

HEATHER PSYCHIC (10:42 AM): Lol.

HEATHER PSYCHIC (10:43 AM): Did you feel any strange side

effects? Lethargy, a sudden cough, inability or difficulty of breath? Besides, you know, normal not having breath after a kiss, if that's a thing?

Grace blinks at her phone.

GRACE (10:44 AM): No none of that.

HEATHER PSYCHIC (10:44 AM): Good! He wasn't trying to sap your life force then.

Because of course that is a thing. Because of course in a world that has ghosts, they also have ghosts that try to drain life force by kissing people, and it's never a thing she thought she'd have to worry about before.

DEBORAH (10:45 AM): I'm still in Kansas, but I just got a call from a Mike asking about you.

And immediately, the feeling of being able to concentrate and think on something else craters, and she sits down on the floor hard next to her box.

DEBORAH (10:47 AM): I faked not knowing you and told him that if he called again I'd call the police.

A bubble bursts from her chest, right as her phone makes a completely unfamiliar beep.

Trixie pokes her head out from behind a bunch of wiring equipment to raise an eyebrow at her.

Grace fumbles around with her phone, until she realizes that the alert is coming from her alarm system she set up with Rodrick, and her stomach drops.

"Oh no," she mutters.

She flips open the apps for the interior cameras, and one is very clearly broken, covered by some sort of material, and the other one, the one that faces her industrial stove, just shows a few tall men with their backs to the camera, huddled around her table.

"Fuck," she breathes, clenching her fist around her phone.

"What now?" Trixie says, ducking her head back into the electrical equipment.

Grace pushes herself up, giving a critical look to the box. "Just got a semi-important text I need to go home to take care of," she says, shying away from the subject matter, because if she has to say what it's for then Trixie will make a big deal of it and...and she doesn't want that. Just firmly doesn't want that with all of her being. "I'm gonna take a lunch now, this'll finish drying while I'm gone?"

Trixie pokes her head back out to give her a flatly unimpressed look. "You need to drive all the way out to Rialto for a semi-important text?"

Because of course she's more intuitive than that.

"The alarms went off at my house, and I need to reset them," she half-bluffs, hating herself, just a bit, for being too scared to tell Trixie at this moment.

"The alarms went off and you're not, I dunno, calling the police?" Trixie asks, grabbing her sweater. "I'll come with."

"No, no, it's okay, it could be dangerous," Grace says, then squeezes her eyes shut at such an obvious faux pas. "I mean, it's probably nothing, it's probably just some faulty wiring because it's an old as fuck building, but on the chance that it is something, I don't think you want to be there when it happens."

Trixie gives her a blank, uncomprehending look. "And you do?"

"I want'..." she trails off, because what the fuck does she want. "I want my stuff to be safe, and I know how to handle this."

"Yeah, don't care, I'm coming with. Unless you're getting a police entourage, which I would encourage." Trixie shoulders her purse and follows her out to the truck.

Her phone makes the alert again, then again, Rodrick desperately trying to get in contact with her that they're there, and in their rush to put it in place they did nothing to make it so she could give him at least a message received.

As they drive the hour drive to Rialto, Trixie remains silent, only texting and speaking to say she notified their work site and a friend of hers on where they were going to be, in case anything happens.

Grace takes out her phone, hands shaking, and makes the obligatory, "I think my alarms went off, I'm going to check them in case it's anything" call to the police, the futility of it sitting in her stomach poorly.

~

THEY PULL UP, and the police she called are outside her door, chatting genially with Mike and a nameless goon with long hair.

Trixie exhales, hard, when she sees the police being so friendly. "Man, you weren't kidding." She bites out, the generally friendly expression on her face turning into something hard and sharp.

"Yeah they're probably cousins or something." With a decisive turn of her key, she turns off her truck, steeling up her back to go over and deal with whatever the hell this is.

The police officer waves her over, generally kind and slightly pudgy looking. "You call this in?" At least his voice isn't at all judgy, just inquisitive.

She nods, and Trixie appears behind her, a fearsome look on her face. "I got an alert that an alarm was tripped, so I checked my security cameras." She instantly becomes aware that she's the only non-white person standing there, so she puts on a big, customer service smile.

The police officer nods, seemingly understanding. "These men claim you gave them a key to come in to install wiring?"

Grace snaps her eyes up to Mike, who just looks smug. "Nope, I do all my wiring myself, I'm a construction and design specialist," she says.

" I was on a work site with her when she got the alert, and when she accessed her security cameras." Trixie chips in.

"Sorry ma'am, my boss must've given me the wrong key," Mike chimes in, giving her a winning smile.

"No one else has my key," Grace snaps, then pastes the smile back over her face. "Sorry officer, I've had a stalker before, I'm very concerned with this sort of thing."

The officer's eyebrows raise at the back and forth. "Miss, you claim you haven't given out your key?"

"Changed the lock when I bought the property, I am on site for any deliveries or contractors, I keep a detailed log of all coming and goings, and these men have been harassing me at my workplace for weeks." She finishes off, her heart pounding.

A quick glance inside her doors show Rodrick standing there, staring out, as if willing himself to be able to see her.

Mike immediately turns to the police officer. "Gerry, I have never seen this woman before in my life, it was just a wiring gig, I can have my boss pull up the work order."

"You have seen her, you showed up to our lunch last week!" Trixie snaps out, then straightens, all official and fury. "I can be a witness to that," she says, cold.

The police officer checks with Mike, and, after a moment, consults his notepad. "I'm going to need to see that work order, sir." And his voice is still friendly.

Mike produces paperwork, because of course they printed out something, and they did it with enough foresight to print a slightly wrong address, to give them cover.

"I think that building's empty, it's over there." Grace points, and the police officer gives her such a look, a look that boils over into the pit of fear and rage in her stomach and gives way to despair that this would ever be taken care of.

Mike gives her a smile, the sort of smile that suggests that she hasn't seen him beat a man's head in for defying his boss before. "Sorry ma'am, I must've gotten mistaken."

And the police officer buys it.

AFTER SHE AND Trixie writes up a statement, Grace tests out her locks, cause at least this time they picked them instead of breaking them.

The moment she steps inside, she sees Rodrick's shoulder's slump with relief, and he immediately puts his hand on her arm, as if reassuring himself that she's okay, before he stiffens when Trixie steps over the threshold.

Trixie and her share a look, before Trixie rolls down the interior door behind them. "We should get you some electronic locks, how about?"

"Yeah, something that can't be picked." Under the pretense of looking around, she locks eyes with Rodrick. "Thank god for my alarm system."

Rodrick's face creases, and he nods at her, his hand on her arm, much more for himself rather than her, and despite the awkwardness of whatever the hell it was the previous morning, he doesn't disappear.

Trixie looks around, and the place is somewhat of a mess. Papers everywhere, her construction contracts spread over her table, and clothes from upstairs draped on the railings of her loft. "How that officer didn't...I dunno...look at this and not immediately think a break in?"

Grace's stomach drops, cause now all of her future jobs lined up have the possibility of them just showing up. "Police tend to believe the clean cut red headed guy over the woman dressed in construction clothes, especially if they talk to them first," she says, gathering the paperwork before craning her neck to her loft.

"Seriously, it's like they just threw things everywhere."

Rodrick nods, feverish. "They stole some clothing," he says, his face twisting.

Of course, Trixie doesn't hear any of that. "Do you keep any jewelry anywhere? We might..."

"Yeah." She turns to go up the spiral staircase, and Rodrick follows her, the hand on her arm still.

"They didn't take jewelry, I can tell you everything just..."

She nods, hopefully subtly, and he gets it, huffing his cheeks out.

Her loft is...a mess. Clothes everywhere, paperwork everywhere, her mattress stripped.

Trixie clatters up the stairs behind her, and her eyes go as wide as saucers as soon as she sees the chaos. "Jesus, do you have something they were trying to get?"

"Clothes," mutters Rodrick.

"Probably trying to find any hidden sources of money and take it from me, if I had my guess," Grace says, her mouth going on autopilot. "I mean, they've done that to people before just...not me."

Trixie gives her a narrowed eye look, before again looking out at the chaos. "I never thought that I'd say this, but man, fuck the police."

"Yeah they're not the best." Grace nudges some of her clothes with her foot. "Um, I can drive you back, but I kinda need to deal with this..."

Trixie waves a hand. "I'll Uber."

"We're like an hour out of LA, that's insane." But still, Grace feels that shame of hoping that she can just get out of her hair and she can figure out what happened. And then cry, probably.

Trixie just raises an eyebrow at her. "Yeah, not gonna sweat it, I'll just write it off as a consulting gig on the taxes." She hesitates. "Unless you need me to stay? I can totally stay, I'll just have to let them know. But like..."

"I can call my sister," Grace fibs. "And I have a shotgun. And indoor padlocks for when I'm here."

"Okay good." Trixie nods awkwardly, before calling up an Uber and leaving.

As soon as she leaves, Rodrick turns into Grace, all but burying his head in the crook of her arm. "They took a scarf, some underwear, and a bra," he mumbles, before pulling her down the stairs to the laptop.

He's pale, even more so than, you know, his normal ghost-ness, and everything feels awful and she doesn't want to argue, so she pulls up the Word doc, now with pages and pages of one sided dialogue between them.

I DON'T KNOW HOW THEY ENTERED THE DOOR, JUST THAT IT OPENED AND THEY WERE HERE.

"Probably picked the lock, I think."

He nods, and she can see the white of his eyes along all the sides as he pokes at the keyboard.

THEY WERE TOLD TO LOOK FOR BANK NUMBERS AND RECEIPTS.

And while she had plenty of receipts hanging around, she keeps all her banking info on herself because of this exact reason.

"Rey controls people through money a lot, so that's not surprising."

He presses against her, shoulder to shoulder.

THEY SEARCHED IN ALL FURNITURE. LEFT YOUR SHOTGUN, THOUGH THEY JOKED ABOUT IT.

"Figures."

TOOK YOUR CLOTHING AS A JOKE. THEY WERE LAUGHING.

Out of instinct, she drapes an arm over his shoulders, and he turns away from the laptop to lean into her.

"Are you okay?" And it's a weird sort of echo from early as hell this morning.

But he's literally a ghost, and literally just had the only place he can exist be violated, turned upside down, by a group of people who only wish ill on the resident, the only person who can see him.

He nods into her shoulder.

"Did they leave anything?"

He shakes his head, before pulling back, his lips twisting. He opens his mouth, as if to talk, then shuts it abruptly.

She keeps eye contact with him, and his face crumples. "I think one felt me. Saw me. Something," he whispers, and his voice is hoarse and far away.

The hair on the back of her arms rises, prickling down her spine. "Which one?"

"The one with the long hair."

So, not Mike, which is good. She'd put money on the goon being too stupid to do anything, or too superstitious to say anything.

"Well, it's not like they can do anything to you, right?"

He seems to equivocate. "If they have a psychic, maybe."

She scrambles for her phone.

GRACE (2:01 PM): Can psychics hurt ghosts and can we do anything to prevent it?

The three dots appear four times, before:

HEATHER PSYCHIC (2:03 PM): wtf?

Rodrick twitches next to her.

HEATHER PSYCHIC (2:04 PM): Now you're being threatened?

GRACE (2:04 PM) It's complicated, we just think that someone we don't want to might've seen/sensed him.

She sets her phone down, and they both sort of stare at the laptop for a few seconds.

"They made jokes about you," he says, his voice raw, before shaking his head and pointing at the laptop again.

"Talking that bad?" She says, in a half attempt to make a joke and a half attempt to focus on anything besides the fact that Rey had his men in here, in her own house, after all that she had done to try to hide her movements.

He seems to shrug into himself.

I COULDN'T DO ANYTHING BUT STAND THERE.

"I got your alarm, that was something." She pauses, one bad possibility after another hitting her. "Were they planning on staying until I came home? Or just leaving after they found it?"

LOOKING FOR SOMETHING AND THEN LEAVING. I THINK.

She studies him for a second. He's sitting with his legs curled underneath him, his shoulders slumped, and his arms wrapped around himself when he's not actively typing.

He looks withdrawn, drained, like someone took him and wrung him of all his energy.

"Well, I'm glad you told me they where here, now...I dunno...if I call the police again they'll have a track record of everything going on. It won't just be one time."

He blinks at her, as if becoming aware of her all over again.

"I know, they don't help the first time. Sorry." On impulse, she reaches out and rubs his arm, in the most basic soothing treatment ever. "Wish they didn't come in here."

He opens his mouth again, closes it, then visibly grits his teeth. "They broke in, not you."

The difference -- and the fact he sees the difference -- warms her a bit. "Well, next I'll have to buy a fucking electronic lock, isn't that just great."

He rolls his eyes, and the slow terror of the day melts, just a little, before he leans in again. But, instead of the awkwardness that it probably should be, it's just...nice.

"How'd...how'd the police deal?" He says, slowly, deliberate after a long pause, as if forcing himself to speak and not use the laptop. "Your friend said..." he trails off.

"They told the police they were here for a wiring company, the police believed them."

His eyes narrow.

"I know, it's bullshit. They forged a work order that they were authorized to enter."

"They had no key."

For a split second, she wonders if he could hear the scraping of the lock picks at the door, and if he knew what they were.

"They claimed they did, the police were officially looking into it."

Her phone buzzes once more.

HEATHER PSYCHIC (3:22 PM): Can I come over? I might have a few ideas and I want to run them by you and Rodrick before I just suggest some things.

She looks over at him, and his face twists and he hunches over. "Okay. And I do not try to suck life force from people."

So he had read the earlier texts. "I wanted to double check, it's not like I've been kissed by a ghost before."

"You might've, you just might not've known," he points out, and the switch of subject seems to make talking easier for him once again.

"That's not helpful," she points out, and he gives her a small smile. His shoulders are still slumped and he still looks pale, but it's a smile.

~

BY THE TIME Heather gets there, Rodrick is unwound and leaning solidly against her, in a way that seems less like some sort of wispy pressure and more, if she doesn't think about it, like an actual person. Like, if she closes her eyes and doesn't think so hard, she can imagine that he's someone she met off the street and brought back to her place, never mind that that is not something she'd even remotely do. But still.

The electronic chime of the doorbell makes her stiffen, before she pulls out her phone and shows Rodrick the camera.

Heather stands there, with two duffel bags and three scarves, looking just as shifty as she always does.

Rodrick pokes at the phone, of course going through it, but doesn't seem troubled by it.

"This is how I can check who's coming to the door when I'm not home," Grace says, slow. "I'm gonna get a lock that can back it up so I can unlock from far away."

He nods, solemn, not getting up as she rises and crosses to the padlocked doors, rolling them up and letting Heather in, before rolling them back down and padlocking them.

Heather raises her eyebrows at the utter fucking mess, before drawing her brows together and giving her a sharp look. "Did Rodrick do this?"

"No," Grace says, shaking her head. "A break in."

Heather's eyes track from the clothing strewn over the place clearly from the balcony, to the papers, to everything. "Well."

With a glance to and fro, like she's trying to place where Rodrick is, she sets the duffel bags on the long dining table, unzipping them with something resembling panache.

"So I did research," she says, before falling silent and pulling out a large binder, its pages all in plastic sheet protectors.

Afterwards she pulls out some comically large markers, the sort you use to paint on car windows, and a box of matches, but doesn't continue talking.

A look of profound curiosity crosses Rodrick's face, and he unfolds himself and walks through the couch to the table, where he stands pressed against Grace.

Despite the weirdness and the adrenaline of the day, it feels nice.

Something that she could relish and feel good about herself for. Something solid and very real and very nice.

"What sort of research?" Grace asks, as soon as it becomes clear that she's not continuing to speak. Or, rather, that she forgot to follow up her sentence with the logical conclusion.

Heather blinks at her, her large eyes wide, before nodding absent-mindedly. "On the idea of protecting the ghost from wayward psychics," she says, as if explaining to a young child. A young child she's fond of, of course, but still a young child. "These, Grace, are Runes."

She spreads the binders open, and the glossy pages are full, absolutely full, of shapes and squiggles and esoteric lines after esoteric lines.

Next to her, Rodrick twitches, but his face is still perfectly curious.

"They're in the laminate so they don't affect anyone I don't want to. Or, rather, anyone that doesn't want to." Heather says, as if that makes sense. "And most of these are for magical beings and not just run of the mill psychics, but still, the principal still stands."

Grace exchanges a look with Rodrick, who shrugs. "I don't know them," he says, his voice just above a whisper. Like he did all his talking earlier and could only summon up the energy for a small volume. "They all look like nonsense."

Heather shifts from foot to foot. "He was talking, wasn't he? That's what that just was?"

Rodrick gives her such a dirty look that Grace cracks a smile. "He said he didn't recognize anything."

"Well, yeah, it's all stuff you need an education on, and I really doubt that it was common knowledge for factory workers in the Great Depression," she says, offhand. "I mean, I don't know most of this, and I work in this. That's why we have dictionaries."

She unlocks the binder and opens it with a satisfying clack, pulling out a section of pages.

"What I'm curious about, what I really want to know, is if you feel anything when I pull them out," Heather says, her eyes unfocused in the general direction of Rodrick. "Anything that makes you feel uncomfortable, for any reason, let us know. These are all generic protection runes, and I don't want them to think that you're one of the things that needs protecting from."

Rodrick's eyebrows raise at being so clearly spoken to.

"I went over them with my coworker, she doesn't think anything will harm you cause, well, you've been in this place for longer than it has, but still you know." Heather spreads the pages across the table, page after page of strange drawings, like the things found on occult TV shows.

"Why didn't you use these at that thrift store?" Grace asks, poking through the plastic sheets. "Wouldn't that be easier than the sachets?"

"No," Heather says, her voice off and dreamy. "Runes aren't too good at stopping things already there, just stopping things from happening in the first place." She holds out a single page, one that Grace can see no difference in from all the rest, expectant. "Rodrick, do any of these bother you?"

He cranes his neck and makes as if he is going to grab the page, but of course his hand goes right through it.

"Set it on the table?" Grace says, rubbing the bridge between her eyebrows. "It'll be easier to read?"

Heather hesitates, then slides it out of its plastic cover and slips it onto the table.

With a wary glance to Grace, he leans over, peering over the page like someone would look at a map of hostile territory.

"I don't like this one," he whispers, pointing at the second on the list. "I don't know why, but it makes my skin crawl." His hand moves to the one right next to it, like he's referencing information in a giant book. "This one is fine, I think."

Grace relays that to Heather, whose face brightens and she scribbles a note in her notebook.

"So that one makes it so you can't be brought to weakness by a simple spell," Heather says, still scribbling in her notebook. "Something that some psychics do is sorta blast spells around, so they can just sorta neutralize anything weird around them. Like spraying pesticide."

Rodrick and Grace exchange a glance at that.

"That sounds lovely," Grace says, after it becomes somewhat apparent that Heather is expecting a response.

"Oh it's fully unethical." Heather pushes her glasses up with her pen, barely pausing in writing. "I mean there aren't really any laws against psychics doing stuff but that's looked down on and all, but if these guys ransacked your place like this..." She gestures at the dirty laundry everywhere. "I'm gonna venture to guess they won't be nice about spells.

With a nod, Rodrick turns back to the spread out pages.

He runs his hands, tentative, over the plastic covered pages, like he could caress them into being solid for himself, his face pensive, and Grace feels herself drawn to his hands.

When he's visible like this, when every part of him is visible, every hair on his arm and every vein on his skin, it's the most surreal. Like he's a boy she could take home to mother, to go on dates and drinks with. Like he's just as real as she is, as Heather is.

But his hands even show small marks, the sort of calluses that come with hard work, and the sort of scars that come from a life of nicks and scratches. Small crisscrossing lines of a life well lived, and knew how to work.

It's sobering, the thought.

Heather eyes the rough space where he's at somewhat warily, as if still expecting some sort of bad reaction from him, but she soldiers on anyways.

"If you feel comfortable with it, I can mark up the place now?" Heather says, and Grace isn't sure who exactly she's asking. "I mean, that one needs to be just put under an entry rug really."

Rodrick nods offhandedly, and Grace nods as well. "He says okay."

With a raised brow at her, Rodrick meets her eyes with his ice blue ones, and she can see the stress lines across his face. "If that's fine with you," he says, his voice muted, and all of a sudden all she wants is for him to not have to do this, to be able to sit down and rest and recover from the day and all the shit and all the intrusions.

So she nods sharply, looking over the runes as well.

They're all foreign to her, none of them provoking a response. Rodrick watches her, still in only the way he can be, before he forcefully exhales and places his cool hand over hers.

All at once, it's like the scribbles on the page raise themselves, like she's reading Braille, and the hair on the back of her neck sticks straight up.

Gentle, he guides her hand over to the one he picked just moments before, and it's like it warms her hand, generating small heat. Like a phone that's been used for too long, like a laptop with a bad fan, or a light shade that's a hair too dusty.

"Oh," she says, blinking, her eyes watering for no reason.

Out of the corner of her eye, she sees Heather looks up sharply, but too much of her attention is on the runes.

"This is what I mean," Rodrick murmurs, very close to her ear, and it's all of a sudden very intimate. "It's strange."

She nods, still blinking rapidly, as he brings her hand to the one he rejected, and it's like dousing her hand in antifreeze. Cold, slimy, and somehow toxic feeling. Like it drips off of her slowly, coagulating on the way down, before he pulls it away.

Without saying anything else, he lifts his hand off of hers, his eyes lingering on her face.

The moment is heavy, like something has happened that she hasn't quite realized yet, and she shivers for a second before shaking her shoulders loose.

He points to another one, his brows drawing together.

"Uh, Heather, what is this one?" Grace asks, and her voice doesn't quite break, but it's a close call.

Her eyes much sharper than they've been on all other times, Heather barely even looks before answering. "It makes it so the ghost can manipulate a negative psychic."

That hangs in the air.

"It means, if someone comes in with bad intentions, Rodrick can...shove him. Or something. Makes him solid-ish to Rodrick."

"That one," Rodrick whispers, his voice faint. "I'd like that one."

Grace nods to Heather, who raises an eyebrow, before scribbling it down as well.

RODRICK DISAPPEARS for a bit as Heather silently scribbles the runes under her entry mat, then another one behind every door of the cabinets, leaving Grace to halfheartedly pick up her laundry, until Heather straightens with a somber look on her face.

"Don't know why you're gonna need all of this, but seriously, take care of yourself?" Heather says, her voice tentative. "I mean, I know about the gun, but like...do you have other plans?"

Grace gestures at the markers in Heather's hands.

"Grace, this only works on like... point-oh-five percent of the population." Heather's voice dips low, like she's worried about someone overhearing in the cavernous warehouse. "If they're trying to hurt you, should you..." She trails off, and it just might be the most tentative she's ever seen her. "Do you have a safety plan?"

The last bit, blurted out, makes Heather turn bright red.

Grace regards her for a quick second, cause that word choice is very particular and one that very few people actually use.

"Well I have my sister--I'm going to be inviting her to stay on a few bad nights," she replies, slowly. "We've set up a wire for Rodrick to let me know if someone's here, and...the gun."

Heather nods slowly as well. "And the police aren't useful."

The way she says it, there's some certainty in her words, as if she's experienced it as well.

"Not always, no."

There's a long moment, awkward, before Heather nods once more, as if she's so uneasy she wants to jump out of her skin. "I gotta go, I will see you later? Text if you need me? Or backup?" With that, she all but runs to the door, as if scared that the conversation will go any further.

Which, fair, neither of them want to do that in that moment.

The moment Grace rolls down the interior door again, Rodrick appears, close to her elbow but carefully not touching her.

"Oh, hi, you're back," Grace says, weary, her hands aching as she padlocks the gate. "I take it the runes don't hurt?"

He shakes his head, his eyes clear and alight, as if he's much more hyper than she feels.

He follows her, not speaking, but he has a spring in his step, as she haphazardly tries to pick up as many papers as possible from the storm of them strewn all over. Exhaustion seeps into her, like too much has happened that day, like too many things have hurt her. Like too much is going on.

"The legal thing is in three days," she says, out of a lack of anything else to say, the dizzying silence buzzing around her skull. "At ten AM. I'm not...I'm not going."

He nods, as if he expected that.

"I'll call my sister, she'll be here for after. She's getting back from Kansas that morning."

He nods again, but this one is more reasoned, slow.

"I'm sorry...I'm sorry they came in here."

At that, the light in his eyes dims a little, but he nods, before reaching out and softly touching her arm.

That touch, that little touch, makes her breath catch in her throat, like it's worth so much more that she's putting into it.

Watching her, moving slow, as if gauging her reaction as carefully as he can, he takes a deliberate step into her personal space.

Her breath escapes her, quiet and quick, and this close she can see the soft small hairs on his cheeks, the movement of the not-blood in his veins, and feel the now soothing chill come off of him.

This close, his eyes dart down to her lips, then back up, clearly and quietly asking for some sort of permission.

And there he waits, a hair's breadth away from her, still as only he can be, clearly waiting.

Exhaling, slow, she reaches up and grips his other arm back, and he's solid under her touch. Solid, real, and she feels any small edifications inside quickly crumble.

"Is this okay?" She blurts out to him, and he wrinkles his brow at the question before breaking out into a smile.

Quiet, still quiet, he leans forwards and presses a kiss against her lips, then one on each cheek, as if that's more intimate, as if there's more he wishes to convey than just the singular kiss.

Her skin tingles where his lips press, and her stomach turns over.

But not in a bad way. In the way that her skin feels like she's finally able to settle into it. Like she's been all over the place and she can finally sit down at home. Like her mind's been racing and she's finally come to the proper conclusion, and she can rest.

Her eyes fluttering shut, she leans forward, leaning into him. His hands brace her, and their lips meet again, even more gentle than before.

It's not like she's stupid, or like she's had no other kisses besides Rey, she knows how to tell if she's being foolish. She knows how to not throw herself at the first man who shows something resembling affection. She knows that comfort is not the same as safety, and is not the same as anything resembling secure.

But damn if this isn't nice. Damn if this doesn't make her sink into herself like a contented cat. Damn if it's not exactly what she wants right now, on the eve of whatever the hell is going on legally, with the break in and the intimidation and...

He breaks the kiss into a whisper, a bare movement of his lips against hers, and she can barely hear him.

"What?" She whispers back, as if they'd be overheard where they are.

Leaning his forehead against hers, his eyes squeeze shut, and he kisses her again, instead of answering.

They kiss like this, soft, chaste, and sincere, and his hands wind into her hair, soft and never pulling, until he steps away in a tender motion, leaving her head swimming.

They regard each other, Grace feeling slightly solemn, but not...bad. Serious, but not bad. Not stressed. Her heart's not pounding, not like the way it used to after Rey, not like it does when she thinks he might be just like him.

He breaks the moment, just a bit, reaching his hand out to hers, holding it silently, before he nods, and disappears, leaving her to quietly walk up the steps to her loft bedroom and falling into her bed.

LATE THAT NIGHT, maybe early in the morning, she rolls over and peers down at her warehouse, and Rodrick is sitting in the over-stuffed armchair, looking lost in his thoughts.

She smiles at him, but he's still, not looking up at her, but still, her heart feels a little better inside at the sight.

13

The day of the legal event, her sister knocks at her door promptly at eight thirty in the morning, and Grace has been awake for three hours at that point and is full of jitters and coffee.

Deborah doesn't quite purse her lips at her, but it's a very near deal, as if she can tell her sister's been making questionable life choices and kissed a dead guy.

But instead, Deborah just watches as she rolls down the interior door and padlocks it behind her.

"So you're staying here all day?" Deborah says, making her way to the couch and flopping over on it, not even bothering to kick off her boots.

Rodrick appears for a split second to give her a disapproving look before vanishing again, and Grace has to swallow down a laugh.

"Well, I don't want to be out there." She gestures broadly. "And if I'm here I can padlock myself inside and call the police."

Deborah gives her a look like she's not sure if she approves or not, but the look also says that she doesn't really want to bring it up regardless.

"Do you think they'll come straight here?" Deborah asks, and Grace gets it. All of a sudden, she gets it.

Deborah mostly lived across the country when Grace was dealing with the worst of it, when Grace had the original court case and the threats and the running in fear. And, therefore, Deborah didn't have that much hands on experience with dealing with the nitty gritty scary parts of this. Of the people showing up and the veiled threats and the police not being effective.

"Well, if they do it'll be pretty hard for them to get through that when it's on this side." Grace points, before sitting on the opposite side of the couch. "And if they do, I have some guns."

Again, the side eye of the disapproval. "Have you actually shot the gun at a person?"

"Not at someone, but certainly pointed it."

Her sister makes a discontented sigh, the sort of sigh that masks a lot of anxiety behind a veneer of annoyance. "Well, can I at least help clean? Or something? I don't wanna sit on my ass all day just waiting for something bad to happen. It looks like a tornado hit here."

And yes, while Grace did her best to clean over the last few days, the place still bears the general sheen of something gone horribly wrong.

"Yeah they tossed my place a few days ago, it was bad," she says, way more flippant than she feels.

Deborah skyrockets to a sitting up position. "They were here?"

"Looking for banking info we think." She gives her sister an appraising look, really hoping she doesn't freak out. "And took my underwear, but I got them to leave."

"Jesus Christ." Deborah thunks her head back. "Okay, yes, lets clean this place. Jesus." As if it pains her, she peels one limb off of the couch after another, laborious. "I get to veto your next boyfriend."

She's hardly the only person who has said that, so Grace shrugs it off and stands as well.

FOUR HOURS after the court time, they can hear three cars pull down their driveway, idling outside.

Deborah gives Grace a pale faced glance, before twisting the volume of the music up. Her hands shake, and Grace desperately wishes she never dated a guy that would scare her sister so much.

Grace grabs the shotgun from its umbrella rest, then stalks over to the opposite side of the warehouse, not really wanting to be super close to the door.

As if summoned, Rodrick appears, peering near the door, his ice blue eyes trained unerringly at the lock.

Despite the music, they hear a car door open, then slam shut again, and the exterior door rattling.

"They broke the outside lock. I'll be getting an electronic lock shortly," Grace says, as if narrating this will make it better.

Deborah sits in the far corner, on the fluffy rug right next to the oversized chair, curling her legs up and hugging her knees. "Do you think they're armed?"

Grace flops onto the chair, holding the shotgun limply with one hand. "I mean, probably. The odds are in favor of that."

Leaving his post at the door, Rodrick strides over to them, and the cool presence is a nice, small bit of relief in the almost overwhelming pressure of anxiety. In response, she flickers on the grounded lamp, and he stands under it.

Her sister's eyes don't leave the door, but she scoots so she's sitting with the chair between her and the door, and, trying desperately to not freak her sister out, Grace dials the police.

The door rattles again, audibly, as Grace tells the police what's going on, and they promise to send someone over. She can hear the gasp as the operator hears the door through the phone.

Coolly, Rodrick slips a hand onto her shoulder, and she glances over at him.

"The psychic's here," he says, whispering, despite the fact that her sister won't be able to hear him no matter what. But like the moment needs whispering, as they all but cower in this far corner. "He brought something, it smells bad."

So it's a good thing they got Heather to do the runes. Grace exhales hard, and they wait.

After fifteen excruciating minutes, the red and blue police lights reflect through the high windows, and that muscle between Deborah's shoulder relaxes. Because she still believes that police are the good guys.

In this case, regardless, they can't hear any specific words, so they just watch the patterns of the lights against the far walls, until they hear the car doors slam again, and the cars drive away.

Slowly, her hand not wanting to unclench, Grace sets the shotgun on the floor, and her fingers ache from holding it for so long.

"Is that it?" Deborah asks, her voice wavering.

"For today, maybe."

Grace stands, and her legs are just as tight and as achy, but she ignores the pull of her muscles and crosses to her fridge, pulling out two beers and handing one to her sister.

Despite it only being around 1 PM and her usually being a snob about these things, Deborah takes the beer and downs it in one go.

Without speaking, Grace pulls out another one and sets it in front of her sister, and Deborah cracks a smile.

Then, despite the situation being really fucking dire and really fucking awful, Grace feels a bubble of laughter in her throat, and Deborah lets loose a giggle, the sort of giggle that's usually reserved for schoolgirls and children.

Feeling it crumble within her, Grace puts her head against the counter, and giggles with her.

THANKFULLY, she's at a different work site the next day, one that just wants an entertainment room re-wired and found her through a recommendation, so she shares her GPS location with her sister and heads off to work.

It's easy work, and lonely work, the sort of work that keeps her in business but not the most mentally captivating, so her mind just wanders.

It won't be the last time they try to contact her, for whatever reason, for whatever point, and they know where she lives. They know she has work, steady work, and that, if needed, they can make her life living hell.

They know her mom, know her very well, and now know her work friends. She moved cities, and they found her there.

It makes the small bubble of panic hit her throat, as she's laying on her back under an entertainment center, but she swallows it down.

Her phone beeps, the strange beep of the wire alarm from Rodrick, and she breathes out of her nose, hard, Then opens up the security app and, sure enough, there are four men standing in her warehouse.

The top down view of the warehouse doesn't show her any details of the men's faces, though Mike's bright red hair shows, vivid.

One of the men, in the back, is shorter than the rest, and her heart skips a beat, and she tries to zoom in on her phone, but can't see any more details.

Rodrick trips her alarm, so her phone beeps again, and again, and she's alone in the house wiring an entertainment center, and her heart beats, fast. She sets the phone down, breathing hard through her nose, laying back down in the dust, plugging in the last few wires she had left dangling, before sticking her phone on speaker and dialing 911.

Steadily working, she describes the scene to the operator, who promises to send someone out. She describes, somehow, that she doesn't want to go there alone, and she doesn't feel safe, and it's like she's speaking the words without saying them. Like, if asked later, she wouldn't be able to repeat them. She'd know she said them, but what they were, she couldn't tell you the moment that she got off the phone.

Her hands shaking, she squints hard at her work, because if she can't do anything, she can finish her work.

On her phone, propped up a small distance away, she sees the police join them, sees paperwork exchange hands, and her stomach sours once more. Sees the police leave, and the four men stay.

Because of course.

Because no matter what precedent she set, no matter what she tells them, they'll believe them over her. No matter what. Despite the police record, despite the threats to her, nothing.

Her phone alarm bings again, and again, and again. Because Rodrick is scared, Rodrick has people in his space who have professed harm to him and to her, and...

"Aww fuck," she whispers, before scooting out from under the entertainment center, and dusting off her hands.

They leave two big gray dirt marks on her coveralls, and she stares at them in dismay before shouldering her work bag.

She leaves a note, promising to finish later, and then climbs into her truck, reaching down and touching her shotgun under her seat.

If she's going into this, she's at least going to be armed. Again.

The desperate alarm beeps on her phone again, and again, and she props the phone on her truck dashboard.

The men in the video are all casually sitting on her couch, as if they own the place. As if the deed is in their name and not hers. As if they have a right to it.

For the first time, a bubble of anger disrupts the well of fear, and she peels out of the tiny suburban neighborhood.

ONCE SHE PULLS UP, the doors are splayed wide open, with Mike's little sedan in front, as well as a much, much fancier Tesla, one she doesn't recognize at all, and she stares at it for a few seconds before parking around the back and pulling out her shotgun from underneath her seat.

Quickly, she fires off the old 911 text to her sister then, after a moment of consideration, to Trixie and to Heather as well, before tucking her cell back into her front pocket.

Because she's not going to go into this blind, and she's not going to go into this scared and unwilling to defend herself.

From inside her pocket, the alarm from Rodrick goes off again, and she knows he can't see that she's outside, but she places a calm hand over the pocket, as if that will soothe.

So, for a lack of anything else to do and before her courage fails her, she turns the corner of her building, fully visible from the door and fully visible to those inside.

Inside, standing around her table, is Mike, the two goons from before and...

And Rey.

He looks out at her, lazy, and the only thing that can pop into her mind is that he looks well rested. Well rested, hair nicely combed back, and a less haggard look on his face than the last time she saw him in court.

And after that one moment of weakness, that one moment where she just lays eyes on him and remembers strongly and vividly that she was once in love with this man, she brings the shotgun up to her shoulder, stepping over the threshold but definitely keeping her back to the door.

"Get out," she snaps, and her voice is clear and doesn't quake.

The goons once again blanch and seem to waver, and they seem like much lesser men than the ones Rey used to keep around him.

Rey doesn't even blink. "You shouldn't be holding guns, honey," he says, and his voice is crystal smooth, wrapping up around her like nothing else. "You weren't meant for that sort of life."

She gestures with the gun, and the two goons take a step back, before one -- the long haired one, the one that Rodrick fixates on -- pulls out a small pistol of his own. Because of course they're armed, they're with Rey, and would be there solely to protect him if he called on them to do so.

Her eyes flicker over to the corner, where they set up the wire alarm, and Rodrick stands there, eyes wide, as if he is unable to move. She nods at him, hoping to be subtle, and he nods back, before stalking forward and passing through the long haired goon, who shivers but otherwise doesn't seem to notice.

"I don't want to talk to you, I want you to get out," she says, again, and her voice wavers, because of course she's not going to be able to talk clearly and firmly right now. "I've called the police, I've notified them that I do not want anyone here, and they know where to look if I go missing."

Rodrick's face twists, but Rey's remains impassive.

"We spoke to them, they know it's just a misunderstanding," Mike says, and it's the first time he's spoken since she's gotten here, and she wishes he hadn't. "They won't come back." The finality of that statement, just makes her nose flare and her skin crawl.

"They lied to them," Rodrick says, and her eyes flicker to him again. "If you call again--"

She nods at him, not caring about being subtle, and with her free hand she pulls out her cell phone.

"Of course you're trying again," Rey says, and he takes a step forward.

Towards her.

His hand outstretched.

In a fist.

Without even thinking, Grace fires.

Her aim is wildly off, hitting a chair at the table and shattering it into smithereens, and many things happen at once.

The goons yell, there's a loud bang, and pain blossoms on her hand, and she drops the gun. Rey yells something, loud, and Mike charges at her, hitting her across the shoulders so she stumbles to the ground, before yanking her up by her collar.

Instinctively, hand white hot with pain and her head a bit blank from the ground, she kicks out, and connects firmly with the side of Mike's kneecap, and he crumbles to the hard concrete floor and she jerks herself away.

Her gun lays on the ground, the wooden barrel splintered, and yet, her hand isn't coated in blood, just a brilliant pain on her ring finger, which hangs at an awkward, cruel angle.

And then, with Mike on the floor clutching at his knee and Rey holding a hand in front of the goons, she stares at them, cradling her injured hand.

It's broken, it's obviously broken, and she won't be able to wire or build things or —

Sinister, Rodrick flickers right behind Rey. Not looking at her, not looking at the psychic, but at Rey. Her heart flips, right at seeing them so close together, and she stutters to her feet.

"I said,--" and now her voice quavers, quavers with adrenaline and fear and tears-- "I don't want you here."

Rey's face is white, pale beneath his freckles, a look she hasn't seen on his face since the sentencing trial, and his jaw works as he glances at her hand.

So she takes that moment to look at him, then turns to run, before three more men appear in the doorway, blocking the interior rolling door.

And it's quiet, too quiet, like all her breath has been stolen away from her. Like it's trapped away from her, just like she's trapped in the building and —

One glances at Mike, then nods at Rey. "We heard shots."

Grace backs away, slowly.

"Yes, good instinct there," Rey says, in his even voice, the voice he uses when he's very angry but doesn't want people to know immediately.

Her stomach churns, very much like she's about to puke, but she grinds her jaw together because the last thing she's going to do is give him that sort of satisfaction.

Rey's face creases at something he sees in her, and he reaches out again, this time with the sort of gentle lying hand he used to all the time. "Gracie, please. You need medical care, we will get that."

"Fuck off," she says clearly, her heart hammering. "Fuck off."

And from the ground, where it clattered, her phone starts to ring.

She makes an abrupt move towards her phone, and the goon with the long hair, the possible psychic, the one who fucking shot her own gun out of her hand, takes a step forward and places his foot over it.

She doesn't miss the nod of approval from Rey, but the phone sings on. Probably her sister, maybe Heather, someone who she messaged and...

"They know to call the police if I don't pick up," she says, scrambling around for words, feeling the will to do anything seep out of her with every shock of pain in her hand, every throb. "They know I--"

The goon points the pistol at her again, more confident this time, and she falls silent.

"We don't want to hurt you. You need to come with us," Rey says, as if he is reasonable.

As if cued by him, the goon fires the pistol at her feet. She flinches back, the bullet kicking up concrete and spraying it at her legs.

An intimidation tactic. Shoot a surface they don't care about, to make them think that they will shoot her.

Her phone ringing stops, then starts up again, somehow managing to convey urgency with just the ringtone.

Rey looks disapprovingly at the goon, but she's seen this enough before. Seen them pull this exact same tactic, exact same method. It would send her scurrying, begging for comfort or mercy.

"Grace," Rodrick whispers, and she drags her eyes to him. His face is unreadable, like it so often is, but he looks down at the gun in the goon's hand, then at her, then at the gun.

Not knowing what to do, not knowing how to communicate it, she just nods at him, her throat tightening, before clawing her attention back to Rey and trying to grab her dignity with all her might.

"Leave," she says, her throat already sounding raw, and she takes a step towards him.

Everyone's eyes widen, sudden, and the gun twitches up to point directly at her.

And, hovering half an inch over the guys hand, is Rodrick's hand. Ready to push it aside, ready to stop it from firing, anything.

His finger curls around the goon's on the trigger.

He nods at her, again, as she finally gets it.

"Oh," she says, fully aware that she sounds crazy.

"Oh what?" Rey says, his voice languid, as if he thinks he's winning. "What's got you so--"

She lunges at him, quick, and the goon snaps it up towards her and fires and —

For a second, it's too loud, and Grace's head rings and she jerks back, but no new pain blooms.

And, slowly, blood blossoms across Rey's midsection. He takes a stuttering step back, before his eyes snap over to his goon, whose hands are shaking while pointing the gun at him.

With Rodrick's hand wrapped tight around his, keeping it steady and pointing it away from Grace.

There's a split second, before all hell breaks loose, and Rey looks up at Grace with something resembling detached horror, like she's the one that pulled the trigger and she's the one that caused this and she's the one who hurt him and —

Sirens sound in her ears, as the police finally show up again.

POLICE TURN into paramedics who turn into more police who cart Rey away on a stretcher and question everyone, all the goons and Mike and her, and her sister shows up after a few minutes, and her head swims and her hand hurts and everything is too loud and too much.

Rodrick sits with her, on her couch, his hand cool at her elbow, not saying a word, just being there. When the police question her, he's a steady pressure at her side, and when the paramedics splint her arm, he's holding her other hand.

It's a blur, everything's a blur, and her sister is screaming at the blood and at Mike and at Rey, even as they load him in the stretcher, and she can't feel anything else as she's loaded into a different ambulance and has to leave Rodrick standing at the doorway.

HOURS LATER, so late it's nighttime, she's discharged from the hospital with an impressive cast and the information that the goon confessed fully to trying to shoot her, but missing and getting his boss.

Deborah takes her home in her car, and her sister's still shaking, and she crashes on the couch and falls asleep fast, her neck contorted.

There's a pit in her beautiful concrete floor from where it was shot, and her gun's gone into evidence, and Rodrick's nowhere to be seen until she trudges herself up the stairs to her loft.

He sits on her bed, as if waiting for her, and stands when he sees her.

"You're alive," he whispers, his voice low and thin. "I didn't know what would happen when you left."

She nods, then sits down next to him, pulling him with her good hand down so she can press up against his shoulder.

He throws his arm around her, and she presses her face against his chest. "It's just a few broken bones in my arm," she says, her voice muffled by him, somehow. "I'm gonna be fine."

She can feel him breathe, somehow, and he holds her tighter. "You're going to be fine."

And he holds her there in his arms, until she can melt and float away into sleep.

~

She awakens the next morning to his face, close to hers, his eyes shut, as if sleeping himself.

HER INJURED HAND THROBBING, she stares at him for a long second, but for the first time in a while, she doesn't feel scared.

END

ALSO BY ALESSA WINTERS

The Paranormal Organization Series
Marked By The Demigod
The Succubi's Choice

Summer Reads
The Man of the Lake: A Merman Romance

Follow her on twitter at @writerLyn
Visit her website at: https://wintersalessa.wixsite.com/website

Sign up for her newsletter at: http://eepurl.com/dLfcFw

Made in the USA
Middletown, DE
27 January 2021